dream
of night

Also by Heather Henson

dream of night

heather henson

atheneum books for young readers
new york london toronto sydney

For Caitlyn Dlouhy,
who told me to write about horses.
And for Lila, Theo, and Daniel,
who will ride their own dreams someday.

ATHENEUM BOOKS FOR YOUNG READERS
An imprint of Simon & Schuster Children's Publishing Division
1230 Avenue of the Americas, New York, New York 10020

ATHENEUM BOOKS FOR YOUNG READERS is a registered trademark of Simon & Schuster, Inc.
For information about special discounts for bulk purchases, please contact Simon & Schuster Special Sales at 1-866-506-1949 or business@simonandschuster.com.
The Simon & Schuster Speakers Bureau can bring authors to your live event. For more information or to book an event, contact the Simon & Schuster Speakers Bureau at 1-866-248-3049 or visit our website at www.simonspeakers.com.
Book design by Michael McCartney
The text for this book is set in Bembo.
Manufactured in the United States of America
0211 FFG

10 9 8 7 6 5 4 3
Library of Congress Cataloging-in-Publication Data
Henson, Heather.
Dream of Night / Heather Henson.
p.   cm.
Summary: Told from their different points of view, twelve-year-old Shiloh, a troubled foster child, Dream of Night, an abused former racehorse, and Jess, a woman who cares for both, find healing by helping one another through their pain.
ISBN 978-1-4169-4899-5 (hardcover)
[1. Race horses—Fiction. 2. Horses—Fiction. 3. Animal rescue—Fiction. 4. Foster home care—Fiction.
5. Emotional problems—Fiction. 6. Farm life—Kentucky—Fiction. 7. Kentucky—Fiction.] I. Title.
PZ7.H39863Dr 2010
[Fic]—dc22
2009026213
ISBN 978-1-4424-0611-7 (eBook)

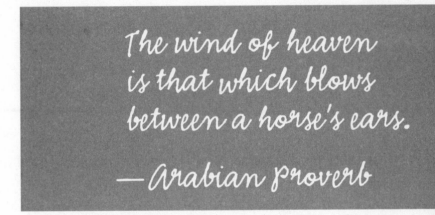

The wind of heaven
is that which blows
between a horse's ears.

— Arabian Proverb

Part one: Rescue

BURDEN, KENTUCKY—*Approximately twenty-five horses were confiscated from a farm here early this morning by the Loyal County sheriff's department after a tip from an anonymous caller. The horses, mares and foals among them, were found in a barn and adjoining paddock, all suffering from severe malnutrition and neglect. The Loyal County Humane Society assisted in the roundup, and the horses were taken to their facilities, where barns are already full from similar rescue operations. They are asking for immediate help in finding homes for these animals. Anyone wishing to foster or adopt a horse should contact the Humane Society as soon as possible.*

One

NIGHT

Brrr—

The sound comes sudden and sharp. Shrill. Like the call of a bird, but not. The sound is not a living sound— somehow he knows that—and it is everything.

rrrr—

The sound is flight, freedom.

nnnng—!

The sound makes his legs move. Before his brain even knows. He is moving. Exploding through the metal gate. Into space.

Not empty space. No. There are bodies in the way, blocking him. But he will move through the bodies just like he moved through the gate. Except he is being held up by the man on his back, and this makes him angry.

And so he fights. And fights. And fights.

To run.

To be faster than the rest.

To be leader of this pack.

To be the winner.

Tight inside the rush of bodies he smells rage and joy. He smells fear. He does not know which makes his legs move faster. All he knows is that he must run.

And so he does. He runs and runs and runs, and around the turn the man lets him go.

A little.

Bodies still in the way but now he can see the empty spaces between them. Because it's the empty spaces that matter in a race. An inch, a moment, a breath to slip through.

Open.

Close.

Open.

Close.

It's that quick. The space between the bodies. Too quick to think about. Time only to move.

And that's what he does.

Move.

One by one the bodies fall away. Until only two remain.

And still the man on his back won't let him go and still he keeps on fighting. It's all he knows how to do.

Fight and fight and fight. And run. As fast as he can

possibly. Run. Just to be the best, the first, the winner of this race.

Nothing to hold him back now. Not even the man on his back. He is faster than the rest and he knows it and the man knows it and so the man lets him go at last.

Two bodies.

One.

Open space.

And that's when he hears it. That's when he always hears it. The sound that makes him run even faster.

A great roaring. Like the wind. Fierce and terrible. And beautiful, too. The most beautiful sound in the world.

Because the roaring means that he is winning, that he is flying.

Dream of Night is flying through air.

Eeeeee!

And then he isn't.

Eeeeee!

Something ripping him out of that time, long ago, when he was a winner. Something pulling him back to where he is now.

Eeeeee!

The ground rumbles and shakes beneath his hooves. Light tears at the darkness. The roaring inside his head has disappeared.

Eeeeee!

He lifts his nose, inhales deeply. What he smells is fear and confusion. Panic.

What he smells is man.

"Hiya, hey! Hey! Hey!"

"Watch it! Whoa, whoa!"

Ears cupping the voices.

None belong to the man with the chains, but it doesn't matter. All men are the same. He hates every one.

"This sure's a wild bunch!"

"You said it."

"Get 'em to go this way."

Now he understands. Men have come to this place, strangers. And the mares are screaming, wild and frantic, to protect their young.

He lifts his head higher, calls out, but the mares can't hear. They are beyond hearing.

And so he stomps his hooves into the hard ground.

Pain like fire burns up his front legs, but he ignores it. He takes a great breath and rears back with every bit of strength he has and lets his hooves smack against the hard wood of the stall door.

Bang!

"Hey, did you hear that?"

"I think there's one over here."

Cupping his ears again, waiting. He knows the men are coming close. He can smell them and he can feel their eyes upon him now, watching through the slats of his stall.

"Getta load of the size of him!"

The voice does not belong to the man with the chains, but it makes no difference. He readies himself.

"He's a big'un all right."

A low whistle.

"I bet he was a looker in his day."

Ears flat back against his skull. Waiting, waiting.

"Not very pretty now. Take a look at those bones! He's starved near to death."

"Last legs, I'd say. Poor old fella."

The scrape of the bar being lifted; the creak of hinges.

He snorts, lowers his head, waiting. A new strength is pulsing though him. The fire in his legs doesn't matter at all.

"Hey there, big fella. How ya doin'?"

It is dark inside the stall but he can see the shape of a man coming forward, hand outstretched.

"Hey there, boy."

Waiting, waiting until the man is close enough.

"Hey, old boy."

Rearing back with all his might. Head up, hooves ready to strike.

"Look out!"

"Get back!"

The door slams shut—just in time.

Hooves striking wood, a hammer blow. Splinters flying into the air.

Bang! Bang!

"You okay?"

"That was close!"

Rising up again for another strike as the metal bar scrapes back into place.

Bang! Bang!

Bang! Bang!

"Whew, what a nutcase!"

"Wonder how long he's been in there?"

"Take a look at that stall. Filthy. I'd be a nutcase too."

He waits now, head low. The air is hard to breathe. The pain is white-hot. But he won't give in.

The men are stupid enough to make another attempt. They click their tongues and talk in soft voices.

He feels only contempt. How can the men think they can trick him with their soft ways? Soft ways to hide the meanness, the need to hurt.

Bang! Bang!

"I think we're gonna need extra hands."

"Yeah, I think you're right."

His whole body is on fire now, flickering, trembling. Still

he kicks and kicks and keeps on kicking. Long after the voices fade away. Long after the screaming of the mares stops and the only sound is the rain, gentle now against the tin roof.

Bang! Bang! Bang! Bang!

Morning light is creeping, dull and gray, outside the barn. It pokes through the wooden slats and falls in faint bars across the dirt floor.

Bang! Bang!

Still he kicks and kicks and keeps on kicking. It's all he can do. Because he cannot run.

SHILOH

Brrrr—

In the shadowy dark the sound is cut off before it has any chance to bloom. Before it has any chance to wake up the old couple sleeping down the hall.

The girl does not say a word as she picks up the receiver and holds it to her ear. Not like she used to, like a dumb baby.

Hello?

And then repeating it. Like a dumb baby.

Hello?

Hello?

Hello?

The first time, years ago, there'd been a click in the middle of the train of wobbly hellos. The sound of dead air. Her own dumb baby voice.

Hello?

Hello?

Hello?

There'd been the tears she couldn't stop.

Hello? Is that you? I know it's you. When are you coming back for me?

There'd been only the dial tone. Nothing else.

And so she learned from then on to be silent. She learned not to cry. She learned to pick up the phone at the first sound and put it to her ear and just listen.

Silence.

That's all. But it makes no difference.

The call is what matters. The person on the other end is what matters, and the day of the year. The one day of the entire year the call will come.

Of course the girl never knows the time. It could be morning or afternoon or night. (Although more often it is night, when other people might be in bed.) Even so, she has to always be on guard, listening, waiting. She always has to be the first one to the phone.

This isn't always possible, in all the different places she's lived over the past few years. One place didn't even have a phone, it was such a dump.

But this place does. The phone is in the kitchen and the old people are down the hall and anyway they sleep soundly through the night. And so when the call finally comes the girl puts the phone to her ear and listens and hardly breathes.

Sometimes if she listens hard enough she can hear a hint of something. The rustle of clothes or the clink of ice cubes in a glass. The sizzle of fire and ash.

Tonight when she closes her eyes she can smell cigarettes, even though the old couple doesn't smoke. She can smell perfume, like candy. Sweet.

When she closes her eyes and smells the perfume and the smoke she can wait. And wait. She can wait forever if she has to, although she hopes she doesn't have to. She hopes one day, if she's quiet enough, there will be a voice on the other end. But for now this is enough.

The girl waits and listens.

Maybe she can hear another sound now. Wet and soft. Steady. Rain? Is it raining there, too?

How far away does her mom live from the old couple's house? How far as the crow flies? Because that's what people say when they mean a place is closer than it seems. As the crow flies.

"W-w-wh-wh-wh . . ."

All at once the noise explodes out of the silence and the girl nearly drops the phone she is so surprised.

"W-w-wh-wh-wh . . ."

Like a siren, a police car coming closer and closer.

The girl knows all about police cars and ambulances. But this sound, it isn't a siren. This sound is human.

"W-w-w-whaaaaa! Whaaaaaaa!"

Somebody is crying.

Not the girl of course. She never cries anymore.

Somebody is crying on the other end of the phone.

"Shhhh-shhhhh-shhhh."

And somebody is trying to shush the crying, stop it before it grows louder.

"Shhh-shhh-shhh."

Getting more desperate.

"Sh-sh-sh-shhhhh."

Somehow the girl knows the "sh-shhing" isn't going to work. She can tell the baby—because that's what it is—the baby is going to rev itself up instead of down, even with the "shhhh-shhh-shhhh"'s. The girl has heard enough babies crying in the places she's been. She's met enough people who must have thought they wanted a baby but didn't when they found out how much trouble they are. When the babies cry and cry and won't stop crying.

"Shhhh! Shhhhhh!"

"Whaaaaaa–whaaaaaa!"

When babies cry like that in the places she has been, people usually tell them to shut up.

"Meet your sister."

The girl clutches the phone closer. Her heart nearly stops dead in her chest.

"A screamer."

The voice is exactly how she remembers. Low and gravelly. From the cigarettes.

"Just like you."

The girl opens her mouth. Is she supposed to talk now? Is she supposed to answer back? What does her mom want her to do?

"Happy birthday, Shy."

Click.

And it's over. Just like that.

One click, and the sound of her mom's voice and the siren cry of the baby (*a sister, she has a sister!*) are gone.

Click.

Like they were never there at all.

JESSALYNN

Brrrrnnnnnnng!

The sound comes from nowhere and everywhere.

Brrrrnnnnnnng!

The woman tries to ignore the sound. She tries to stay in the cozy dark and hold on. To where she is. To the bundle in her arms. But she can't.

Brrrrnnnnnnng!

The sound is already reaching through the darkness, hooking her like a fish and yanking her upward, arms empty.

"Hello? Hello! Jess! Hey, girl, wake up! Jess! Wake up!"

The woman recognizes the voice. Too loud for this time of night—or morning. Is it morning already?

"Jessalynn DiLima! Haul it outta bed, girl! E-mer-gen-cy. I'll be there in thirty."

Click.

Ah, now the woman can return to the dark. Sink back into darkness. Ignore the doorbell when it rings.

E-mer-gen-cy.

Eyes open. Just a squint, but open.

E-mer-gen-cy.

The curtain edge holds the barest hint of light. Rain pattering against the glass, soft and low. A vague memory of something harder, of thunder and lightning deep in the night.

The woman squints at the bright red numbers hovering on the bedside table. Morning, for sure. Way too early.

"I'm going to kill you, Nita."

The old redbone hound dog draped at the woman's feet lifts her head, thumps her long tail once.

"It's okay, Bella. You don't have to get up."

The dark wet eyes have a guilty look. Or maybe the woman is just imagining it. Not so long ago the dog would have been up like a shot, ready for anything. But now there's a dusting of white along her muzzle. The dog's head drops back onto the faded quilt.

The woman sits up and swings her legs over the edge of the bed. She stretches her arms into the air.

"Ahhh!"

A spasm of pain.

Slowly, carefully this time, she tries again, stretching, rising to her feet. Gently she kneads her thumbs into the small of her back.

Mornings mean stiffness now. Stiffness means she's getting old.

"Too old for e-mer-gen-cies at four thirty in the morning," she grumbles, but of course there's no one to hear. The dog, Bella, has already gone back to chasing rabbits in her dreams.

Two

SHILOH

Day breaks and Shiloh pulls the scuffed black canvas suitcase out from under the bed. Everything she owns in the world fits inside. She doesn't even bother folding the T-shirts and jeans and shorts. They're all hand-me-downs or Salvation Army castoffs anyway. Who cares if they are wrinkled?

A faint knock comes halfway through the packing. Shiloh ignores it. She ignores the muffled, fluttery voice, too. The door isn't locked but she knows the old woman is too timid to open it.

When she's done, Shiloh leaves the case where it is on the floor and folds herself into the closet to wait.

Small places are the safest. Easily forgotten.

There, on a low shelf near her head, she sees an old ballpoint pen.

Click, and it's open.

She tests the ink on her palm. And then slowly, carefully, she writes all the bad words she knows on the pure white walls of the closet for the old couple to find later, after she's gone.

The doorbell rings.

Click, the pen is closed. She tucks it into her jeans pocket.

The muffled sound of voices, low and secretive. She knows what the voices are saying even though she can't actually make out the words.

We tried.

Too angry.

Too much trouble.

We're sorry. So very sorry.

Shiloh hates the word "sorry." One of the things she's learned in her twelve years is that people who say they're sorry never really mean it.

"Shiloh?"

The state lady. Just outside the door. Her voice cheerful and bright.

What a fake.

Shiloh yanks the door open. She ignores the fake smile as she walks by. She ignores the old couple sitting on the couch on her way through the TV room.

"Good-bye, Shiloh," the old woman calls in her high,

fluttery voice. "Good-bye. I hope . . ." The voice trailing off, as usual. "Well, I just hope . . ."

Shiloh doesn't wait for her to finish the sentence. She doesn't say anything back as she walks out the door. It doesn't matter. She'll never see the old woman again.

JESSALYNN

Before the pickup even rolls to a stop, Jess is out of the passenger side and making her way toward the paddock. Rain pelts her hard but it doesn't matter. She's used to being out in all kinds of weather. Rain doesn't hurt unless it has some ice to it.

A great mass, dark and muddy, is wedged against the white plank fence. As Jess comes near, the mass breaks apart, screaming and snorting, becoming not just one body but many.

Becoming horses.

Skin and bone. Every one. Barely strong enough to stand, by the look of them.

Still they wrestle with all their pitiful might. Jerking their hooves up from the dark, sucking mud. Stumbling and shrieking, eyes rolling back inside their heads.

Jess takes a slow breath, gazes down at her muddy

boots. The anger rises up fast. The taste of bile sharp at the back of her throat.

It's the same every time. With this kind of rescue. It never gets any easier.

Horses shouldn't look this way. Skeletons with a bit of skin attached.

Horses shouldn't act this way, either. So fearful of human touch they would break off their own legs just to get as far away as possible.

"Oh, Shenandoah, I long to see you."

The singing is a reflex. Automatic.

"Away, you rolling river."

Soft and low. Not really meant for human ears.

"Oh, Shenandoah, I long to see you."

A song her father used to sing when she was a girl. Many years ago.

"Away, we're bound away, 'cross the wide Missoura."

Most times the sound is soothing, a comfort. But not today. These horses are way too spooked.

Screaming and snorting, nostrils flared, the pack manages to pull itself up and away. As far as it can go. Until the thick mud cements hooves in place once more.

"Hey, Jess, this way!"

A voice, calling through the rain and terrible racket.

"They're ready for us."

The voice of "emergency." At four thirty in the morning. With Nita, "emergency" always means horses.

"Foster or for keeps?" Jess hears Nita asking as she comes out of the drizzle into the dry barn.

"Dunno. Court'll decide in a month or so."

Jess can hear the exhaustion in Tom's voice. She can see the dark circles under his eyes when she comes up beside Nita. Tom's in charge of this rescue. He's probably been up all night.

"Can't keep 'em here that long," he continues, waving a clipboard in the air. "We're splitting at the seams. And there ain't enough to keep 'em all fed as it is."

Nita nods. She knows all this. So does Jess. It's the same story, time and again.

A bunch of sickly horses finally get rescued after being mistreated and starved, and the pain and suffering isn't over yet. Not by a long shot. Because there's never enough feed at the Humane Society, never enough hay. Never enough hands to help and never enough homes for the horses to go to.

"I 'preciate you gals coming out like this. On such short notice," Tom says. "And in such great weather, too."

"At least we're not the only ones today."

Nita nods toward the trucks and trailers already lining from the barn to the end of the driveway.

"Yeah, we managed to get it in the papers and on the radio first thing. Word of mouth spreads pretty quick."

"Especially with Nita around," Jess says under her breath. "How many calls did you make this morning, anyway?" She grins over at her friend.

Nita gives a shrug. "I lost track at twenty-five."

"Nita Horne!" Tom cries. "I don't know twenty-five people I could call at this hour of a morning!"

"I don't either." Nita winks. "I just opened up the phone book."

Tom lets out a big laugh. "All right, then, ladies." He taps a thick finger against the clipboard. "First one up is number ten. And she's got a foal."

"Two for one."

"You got it."

Nita turns to Jess, zipping up the hood on her rain slicker.

"You ready?" she asks.

"As ready as it gets nowadays," Jess replies.

The women enter the paddock. Wading through mud, circling, arms fanned out. Trying to get a look at the numbers on the brass tags attached to halters, separate one horse from another, load each one up into a waiting trailer.

All this without stirring up a ripple of panic. Because a ripple builds into a tidal wave. Just like that.

"Whoa! Whoa! Watch it!"

Too late, the black mass senses danger and seizes back. Then forward, surging, a dark sea. Churning and dangerous. Barely missing Jess and another volunteer.

"You're slowing down, old lady," Nita calls over the roar.

"That's what I would've told you this morning," Jess mumbles, "*if* you'd stayed on the line long enough."

The terrified herd settles into a far corner, and the volunteers try it again.

And again.

The rain doesn't stop, and the mud gets thicker. A stew of woman and man and beast. Something out of a movie. A scene in old black and white runs through Jess's head. A man alongside a muddy riverbank, wrestling alligators.

Because that's what this is like. Sorting through this lot is like wrestling alligators. Jess loses all sense of time. And place. Maybe she has been here forever, dodging hooves and teeth. Maybe she has died and gone below, to the place her granny always warned her about.

After a while, though, the sorting starts to inch its way toward easy. Easier. The mares start to give up. Worn out, pure and simple. Broke.

Only the foals stay fierce. Wild. Determined to remain free, untouched.

It's the same every time. With this kind of rescue. The

foals are in better shape than the mares. Because they can still nurse even while their mamas are starving.

And even though she knows one of the feisty, long-legged little foals could kick her in the head if she's not careful, Jess is glad. Just watching the foals makes her heart glad. Because it shows how life goes on. Even in the mud and misery. Life continues.

Another hour slips by, two. Jess ignores the familiar nagging in her lower back, the stiffness in her joints. The only thing that finally stops her is the time.

"Sorry, but I gotta go," she calls to Nita, tapping a finger on her mud-splattered watch. "Got somebody coming at three."

"Which one you taking?" Nita calls back.

"The palomino."

No foal and sweet as pie. Worn out from all the youthful shenanigans. The old gal will fit in fine with Jess's other horses.

"Okay, go get the truck," Nita says. "I'll round her up. Key's under the flap."

Jess nods and heads out of the barn. The rain has let up, but the clouds to the east are still dark, threatening.

Bang-bang! Bang-bang!

A jolt of sound, sudden and close. Like thunder, but not. At least not the kind that comes from the sky.

Bang-bang! Bang-bang!

It's hooves slamming against metal, a new horse trailer pulling up. The kicking going on inside so full of force, Jess half expects to see hoofprints stamping through the walls.

Bang-bang! Bang-bang!

"Whoo-wee, glad we made it!" The driver is jumping down from the cab of the truck. "Not sure the trailer was going to hold."

Bang-bang! Bang-bang!

"Why didn't you tranq 'im?" Tom has come out of the barn with his clipboard. He doesn't look happy.

"We did!" the driver yells over the noise. "He's got enough Ace in his veins to drop an elephant."

Bang-bang! Bang-bang!

"Lord have mercy," Tom says softly. He stands, watching the horse trailer shimmy and shake. "Well, what're we going to do with him now? Where we going to put 'im?"

"You tell me," the driver says, holding his empty palms up.

Bang-bang! Bang-bang!

Jess checks her watch again. She's going to be late, even if loading up the palomino is smooth and easy.

Bang-bang! Bang-bang!

But she can't resist a closer look.

Bang-bang! Bang-bang!

And what she sees through the metal slats makes her

stomach churn all over again. Because what she sees is a shell of a horse, a skeleton, barely alive, but kicking to beat the band. Kicking to show his stuff, to show what he once was.

A Thoroughbred. Jess can see it, despite the thinness and the filthy, rotting coat. A racehorse, most likely. A king, once upon a time.

Bang-bang! Bang-bang!

Nothing but bones now. A bag of bones and skin covered in mud.

Bang-bang! Bang-bang!

And scars. Thick scars winding their way around his neck like a noose. Thinner scars flicked along his sides.

Bang-bang! Bang-bang!

The whip, of course. But chains, too. Jess has seen it before. Willful horses chained to a barn wall to make them mind.

"Listen at that." Tom has come up behind her. She knows he's not talking about the kicking. He's got his head cocked, listening to something behind that. "Pneumonia for sure. Who knows what else. Can't let him get near the other horses. Even if he *was* calm as milk." Tom tugs at his cap, lets out a sigh. "Truth is, I don't know what to do with him. Probably best to put 'im out of his misery." He turns away. "Shoulda done it back there before bringing him all this way, stressing him out even more."

"Now you tell me," the driver says.

There was a time Jess would have protested. Loudly. She would have let Tom have it. Told him how wrong he was. And she would have taken this horse home just to prove her point.

But that was before her back went out the first time, before she woke up with pain and stiffness most mornings.

Bang-bang! Bang-bang!

Before she got old.

Bang-bang! Bang-bang!

Now she's not so sure Tom is wrong.

Out of his misery. Probably the best thing. A horse this bad off, this far gone.

Bang-bang! Bang-bang!

This angry. Jess is about to turn away, nothing she can do, when it happens.

The horse stops. Kicking at his cage. Just stops. And reaches his neck around. Turns his head. To look at Jess.

Is it the singing?

She hadn't even realized. Because it's a reflex, automatic.

Is it the melody?

A song about a river, not a girl. Her father had to explain that to her long ago. Shenandoah is a river, not a girl like Jess imagined. Not a song about love but about longing.

Is it the voice?

Doubtful. Jess knows she doesn't have her father's baritone, which was like an oak tree, deep-rooted, strong.

Whatever it is, the horse is looking at Jess.

And Jess is looking back.

And what she sees she can't explain. Not in words, anyway. What she sees is what this horse once was.

A champion. A king.

Bang-bang! Bang-bang!

The song ends. The moment is gone.

Bang-bang! Bang-bang!

The kicking starts up again. Harder now. Harder even than before.

"What's his name?" Jess asks, turning to Tom.

"Well, he's registered. A money winner, in his day." Tom flips through the list. "Let's see . . . Here we go." He squints up at the trailer. "Nice name. Dream of Night."

Bang-bang! Bang-bang!

"Well, he's nobody's dream now!" The driver spits out a wad of tobacco with the words. "More like a nightmare."

Bang-bang! Bang-bang!

"I'll take him," Jess says, her words getting lost in the noise so that she has to say it again. "I'll take him."

Tom pushes his cap back, looks at her. "I dunno, Jess. Even if he does make it through the night, he's a wild one all right."

"I'll take him." Jess says.

"No offense, ma'am, but you're crazy!" the driver blurts.

"Nothing I haven't heard before." Jess winks at Tom, and he lets out another of his big laughs.

"What about this sweet gal?" Nita asks when Jess comes into the barn to sign the paperwork. She has the palomino ready to go. "She's just a doll." Rubbing her cheek along the mare's muddy neck.

"Can't take both. I've got to go now, and the other's already loaded up."

As if that's the reason. The black horse is already loaded up.

"Thought you weren't taking the hard cases anymore," Nita says, some slyness slipping into her voice. "Thought you were too old."

"I am," Jess answers, checking her watch, letting the second thoughts worm their way in.

What in the world is she doing, anyhow? Taking on a sickly ex-racehorse at this point in her life, at this moment? She's too old, too rickety to handle some crazed-out-of-his-mind Thoroughbred stallion. She'll have her hands full as it is. With the kid coming, this very afternoon—Jess glances down at her watch—this very minute, in fact.

And not just any kid.

"Tough as nails," the social worker said over the phone. "Angry at the world."

Jess studies her muddy boots. The irony does not escape her. An angry kid and an angry horse. Both the same day.

"Where to, ma'am?" The driver has come to find her. He's waiting.

Nita is waiting too.

"My farm's about thirty miles from here," Jess hears herself say.

Bang-bang! Bang-bang!

"Well, let's just hope we make it!"

NIGHT

Nobody's dream now. More like a nightmare.

Because he understands. As all horses do. Human talk.

Although what he knows goes beyond words. What he knows is sound. Timbre. Pitch. Meaning within a sound.

Anger. Arrogance. Fear.

What he knows is smell. The scent every living thing gives off, whether they mean to or not. And the tension, trapped inside the body, betraying the truth behind the words.

What he knows is touch.

The tug of the bit inside the mouth; the jerk of the reins; the sting of the whip.

Touch.

A slap. A punch. A kick.

What Night knows is that touch is something to be avoided at all costs.

Three

SHILOH

The place is deserted. Nobody even comes to the door when the state lady rings the bell.

Grrrrrrrrr!

A low growling starts up from somewhere. And Shiloh freezes. She is terrified of dogs. Although she would never admit it out loud.

Grrrrrrrrr!

This dog is tall and skinny with a short, reddish-brown coat. It slinks around the corner of the porch, mouth open, teeth bared.

"Hello, doggy, hello!"

Shiloh can't believe the state lady is trying to sweet-talk the dog like a baby.

"Hello there, good doggy!"

Shiloh can't believe the sweet talk is working.

"Good doggy, good dog!"

The dog sniffs at the air, wagging its long tail once, twice, allowing itself to be petted.

Not by Shiloh. She only glares when the dog comes her way, sniffing with its long nose and its big mouth full of sharp-looking teeth.

"I'm sure Mrs. DiLima will be here any minute."

The state lady's makeup is starting to run in the sticky heat. And her voice is bright and shiny, as if there's nothing wrong. But Shiloh's on to her. She's learned. After all this time. The state lady's voice gets brighter, more cheerful when things aren't going as planned.

"I know Mrs. DiLima hasn't forgotten about us!" The state lady takes a tissue out of her purse and pats at her forehead.

"Wanna bet?" Shiloh mumbles.

"What's that, dear?"

Shiloh doesn't answer. She hasn't spoken to the state lady all day. She's not going to start now.

"Mrs. DiLima keeps horses. Isn't that neat?"

What Shiloh needs is a pair of sunglasses. For the voice alone.

"In fact, Mrs. DiLima trains horses. She used to give lessons. I bet she'll show you how to ride. Won't that be fun?"

Shiloh turns her back on the state lady. She heads down

the stairs and past the car. Her T-shirt is wet from the rain and then the heat, sticking to the small of her back.

"Stay close, Shiloh!"

A tiny crack in the brightness.

"Stay close, dear!"

Shiloh glances around. Where would she go anyway? The state lady has dragged her to the middle of nowhere. It took forever to get here.

"I'm sure Mrs. DiLima will be along any minute!"

Shiloh kicks the gravel as she walks down the driveway. She stops in front of the black barn because she doesn't know what else to do. The door is open, a giant mouth. It's cooler inside.

Hmmmmm-mmmmm!

A sound trickles out from the darkness.

Hmmmmm-mmmmm!

Like laughter, high and tumbling.

Hmmmmm-mmmmm!

Somebody's inside the barn. Shiloh is sure of it. Maybe it's Mrs. Lima Bean, or whatever her name is, and she's hiding. Maybe she said yes to the state lady, but then changed her mind. It's not like it hasn't happened before.

Sorry.

So sorry.

Too much trouble.

There is a blur of motion in the shadows. Shiloh feels goose bumps up and down her arms. She takes one step back, and then another. When she turns, a truck is pulling into the driveway. Her heart sinks.

Now would be the time. To run. Now. Before she is forced to meet the new foster freak.

But where would she go? How would she find her mom and her sister? (*She has a sister!*) Her mom doesn't live in the old apartment anymore.

"Hello there!" The state lady looks like an idiot, waving both arms in the air. "Hello!"

The truck creeps toward the house, a gray horse trailer pulling behind. Somebody jumps out from the passenger side before the wheels roll to a stop. A woman. Mrs. Lima Bean, probably. And the dog rushes forward, wagging its long tail back and forth, yipping a little.

"Sorry I'm late!"

The woman is wearing a green rain slicker and tall black boots, a black baseball cap pulled low over her face.

"We thought you'd forgotten us!" the state lady says, so bright and shiny, so fake. "We were just waiting here!"

"No, no. Of course I didn't forget." The woman is caked in mud, head to toe. "Had an emergency that went longer than I expected."

"Oh, dear, I hope it's nothing too serious!"

Before the woman can answer, there's a quick blast of sound. Like gunfire.

Bang-bang! Bang-bang!

Shiloh has heard gunfire before. In the old apartment. Before the police took her away. Back then, in the old apartment, her mom would tell her to get down and stay down. And she would.

Bang! Bang! Bang!

Shiloh wants to drop down now. That's her first instinct. But then she knows. It's not gunfire. The sound is coming from inside the horse trailer.

Bang-bang! Bang-bang!

"We need to get him outta there, ma'am," the driver calls, his voice impatient. "You want 'im over in that empty field, right?"

"I'll open the gate." The woman turns back toward the truck.

"I'd reschedule if I could." The state lady sounds unsure. "But it's like I explained to you over the phone—"

"No, no." The woman has her back to the state lady. "This will only take a minute."

Bang-bang! Bang-bang!

"Well, I . . . ," the state lady begins, but the woman has already ducked back into the truck.

Shiloh tries to see what's inside the trailer as it passes by.

Something is definitely moving between the slats. Something dark. And big.

Bang-bang! Bang-bang!

And mad.

"Let's wait on the porch, Shiloh!" the state lady calls out, but of course Shiloh ignores her. She trails the truck—not too close—as it turns past the barn and swoops back around to a red metal gate. The woman and the driver both jump out of the truck and start fooling with chains and bolts.

"You ready?" the driver asks.

The woman swings the gate open, nods. "On the count of three."

"One ... Two ... Three!"

The back of the trailer clatters open, forming a ramp, a bridge from inside to out.

At first there's nothing, only silence. Shiloh scowls. What a letdown.

But then there's a thrumming, deep and steady. Like the beating of a drum. And a streak of black shooting down the ramp and through the gate, across the field.

Shiloh has seen real horses of course. In fields along the side of the road. But she's never seen anything like this. A streak of black, like a dark shadow flying over the grass.

Rrrrhhhraaaa!

And she's never heard such a sound.

Rrrrhhhraaaa!

Like something from a scary movie.

Rrrrhhhraaaa!

Something evil, full of hate.

Rrrrhhhraaaa!

Running, flying, screaming one minute.

Rrrrhhhraaaa!

Stumbling, falling, crashing to the ground silent the next.
Silent and still. Dead.

Shiloh takes a step forward to see better.

The black horse is just a heap of bones, and it's the
woman who's running now. Through the gate and across
the field, the dog following close behind. The woman stops
before the horse. She kneels down, one hand reaching out.

And that's when something shifts. The black heap rises
straight up from the ground. Straight up like a phantom
out of a grave.

And before the woman can get out of the way, the thing
swings its head around and sends her flying.

"Watch out!" the man yells, too late. He runs across the
field, scrambling in the mud to pull the woman to her feet,
get her back to the gate, the black horse and the dog chasing them all the way.

Rrrrhhhraaaa!

Shiloh lets out a laugh. She can't help it. The whole

thing is like a cartoon now. A cartoon of a horse chasing a couple of idiots across a field.

Rrrrhhhraaaa!

The man bangs the gate shut just in time and the black horse lurches sideways along the fence line, blowing white foam out of its open mouth.

"Crazy horse!" the man yells, shaking his head. "You okay?" He turns to the woman. The baseball cap is gone, lost in the mad rush. The woman's hair is loose now, grayish blond, falling to her shoulders.

"I'm fine," she says. "Fine."

But Shiloh can see, even from here, the woman isn't fine. She's holding one hand to the small of her back, and when she moves, it's slow and careful, the way Shiloh's mom always moved when she didn't want anyone to know Slade had hit her.

Rrrrhhhraaaa!

And the black horse is screaming and running again, like a train blasting down a track.

Rrrrhhhraaaa!

Shiloh can't take her eyes off him as he circles the field. She doesn't know anything about horses, but she knows enough to understand how wrong this horse looks.

With his bones sticking out everywhere. And his dark, scaly skin. Scars running along his head and sides. And his giant head with the bulging eyes all red where they should be white. And the foam bubbling out of his mouth. And the weird screaming.

A monster. That's what he is. Inside and out. Shiloh can tell. She knows a monster when she sees one.

"I'd stay and help, but you know how it is back at the barn," the man is saying. "Sure you'll be okay?"

"I'm fine. Thanks for getting us here."

"All right, then." The man hesitates, glancing around at the horse. "Good luck."

The woman nods, but that's it. She doesn't turn or wave. She just stands, watching the horse.

And the horse is watching her back. He has stopped screaming now, but he is breathing hard, head low, staring across the gate. Foam spilling out of his mouth and ears straight back against his skull like horns.

And Shiloh knows. The black horse hates the woman. Hates her, pure and simple. And somehow this makes it better.

The ugly house. The new foster freak. The run-down farm in the middle of nowhere.

It's better now.

Because Shiloh knows something: She isn't the only one who doesn't want to be here.

Rrrrhhhraaaa!

The black horse gives a final scream and turns his back to the woman, swishing his scraggly black tail, as if she is just a fly to be shooed away.

And still the woman stands where she is. Like a dummy. Even though the horse has dismissed her. Obviously. The woman just stands there, with the dog at her side, watching. Holding a hand to her back.

And then she turns, a puzzled look flashing briefly across her face, recovering fast.

"Hey there." She moves forward, slow and careful. "Hey, you're Shiloh, aren't you?" She holds a muddy hand out for Shiloh to take. "I'm Jessalyn DiLima, but you can call me Jess. Most folks do."

Shiloh crosses her arms over her chest, a shield, and finally the woman lets her hand drop.

Up close the woman is ugly, plain and simple. And old. Not as old as the last one, but old enough. The skin around her eyes and mouth is tight and wrinkled at the same time.

But the weirdest thing: Her eyes don't match. Both are pale blue, but the right one is looking at Shiloh while the other kind of wanders off to one side.

"Shiloh. That's a real pretty name."

Shiloh hates this moment. When the foster freaks act like they care. It only happens in the beginning. It never lasts long.

"This isn't permanent."

Shiloh makes her voice as hard as a rock. She wants to scream like the black horse. But this will have to do. For now.

"My mom has a new baby, and she's getting a place ready for me."

The words roll off her tongue. As she speaks, the story becomes true.

"She wants me to look after the baby so she can find a job. That's all she needs. A good job."

One eye is watching her for sure, but one eye isn't. It gives Shiloh the creeps.

"That's great. Really great. I'm glad." The woman smiles, and the smile doesn't make her any less ugly. "So tell me, Shiloh, ever spent much time around horses?"

"No! I didn't grow up on some dumb farm!"

The woman keeps smiling, like a dummy. Maybe she's not right in the head. Maybe she's been banged around by horses a few too many times.

"Well, then." Still smiling, she looks down at the ground and back up again. "We'll take it slow, okay?"

The woman doesn't wait for an answer. She turns and makes her way carefully toward the house, toward the cheerfully waving state lady.

And Shiloh stands absolutely still, watching the woman's

back, wanting to scream. Just like the black horse. So that the woman will know how dumb she is.

Shiloh won't be here long enough to "take it slow." She won't be here any time at all.

Four

NIGHT

A great roaring. Like the wind. Fierce and terrible. And beautiful, too.

The roaring is respect.

The roaring is fresh mounds of hay and more oats than he can eat at one time.

The roaring is a clean, warm stall by night, and a wide open field of grass by day.

The roaring is not there anymore. And yet it is forever.

Caught inside him forever, wrapped inside, deep down, pressing against his heart.

Just like the chains.

Pressing, tightening, until there is pain and more pain. Until there is darkness. And rage.

The chains.

They came later, much later, after the roaring was only inside his head, inside his body. Not outside. Not anymore.

A terrible, beautiful roaring.

Gone now. Mocking. Mocking what he once was.

Dream of Night.

A Thoroughbred. A champion among champions, a money winner, once upon a time.

Big money. Big races. Big crowds. Cheering him on. Roaring from the stands. A cape of roses draped over his body.

Not just once. More than once. More than twice. Many times.

Gone now. Gone forever.

Dream of Night.

Something is draped across his shoulders now. Not the cape of roses. Something heavier, holding him down.

A blanket. He wants to shake it off, but he can't. The pain is too much. Like fire. Not just in his legs. Everywhere.

Who brought the blanket? When did they bring it? While he slept? How long has he slept?

The great horse lifts his head, breathes in the darkness.

Darkness is what he knows. It's what he is. For longer than he can remember.

When the chains didn't work, didn't hold him, didn't make him mind, the darkness did. The stall. The boards nailed up to keep him inside.

How long was that? No food or water? No clean hay?

How long?

Impossible to say.

He's been so long inside the darkness. It is a part of him now. Like the roaring. A part of his soul.

And so he doesn't really believe it at first, when he lifts his head and glimpses something shining, shimmering, high above.

Stars.

Pieces of light. Scattered across the sky.

He'd almost forgotten about stars. And trees. Their dark branches reaching out, always reaching.

He'd almost forgotten about fresh air. How sharp it can be inside the lungs. Painful. Clean. Not the stench of his own excrement. Not the stench of fear and filth blowing in from the other stalls.

Whooo-whoo-whooo?

Ears cupping a new sound, close by, in one of the far-reaching trees.

Whooo-whoo-whooo?

A creature of the dark. The call echoing through the trees.

Whoo-whoo-whoo?

No call answering back. The owl is alone. Night knows about that.

In the barn there were other horses, mares, but he could

only hear them, smell them. He could only catch a glimpse of them through the slats of his stall.

There are horses nearby, in this place. Beyond the fence, inside the barn. He can hear their voices, hear that they are not afraid.

He does not understand. Why they are not afraid. And he does not like what he does not understand.

JESSALYNN

Jess stands in the moonlight, watching from the far side of the fence. The black horse shakes off the blanket, the one she finally managed to drape over his thin frame while he slept. She watches him struggle to rise, shuddering, obviously unable to make his body do what he wants it to do.

Out of his misery.

Maybe she should go ahead and call the vet in the morning. Get it over with. Maybe that's what the look really meant, back at the Humane Society barn, the look that passed between them. A plea for relief, not just rescue.

Jess starts to turn away. But then the black horse makes a sound, low in his throat.

Hmmmmm-mmmmm.

Jess watches as he pushes himself up from the ground,

standing on stiff legs, stumbling a little, unsteady. But standing.

A king. No doubt about it. Way back when. In his early days. A warrior.

Jess holds her breath, waiting to see what will happen next, if the black horse's legs will betray him, if he will crumple back down to the ground.

But no. He stays standing. He lifts his head to the night sky and then lowers it, snorting at something on the ground. The discarded blanket. Kicking at it, trampling it under hoof like a snake or some other varmint he wants dead.

And Jess has to laugh. Quietly, to herself.

Because even though she wishes the blanket had stayed on the horse's back longer, to keep the chills away, to keep the fever down, she has to admire the old boy's toughness, his fight. The only thing that's gotten him through, most likely. The only thing that's kept him alive and kicking in his nightmare of a life. That same toughness, that same fight.

Jess watches a moment longer and then she turns and walks slowly, silently back to the house. She will not call the vet. Not yet. She will give the black horse more time.

Five

SHILOH

The woman is crazy. Plain and simple.

The woman talks to horses.

Shiloh has watched from the window. She has seen the woman's mouth moving. She has heard the woman's voice. Soft and low, so she can't actually hear the words. But she can see. And she knows.

The woman talks to horses.

Crazy. Or lonesome. Or both.

And green. The woman is green at being a foster freak. She doesn't seem to know that most foster freaks treat you like a slave.

Do the dishes.

Do the laundry.

Clean the bathroom.

Watch my snotty kids while I'm gone.

The woman hasn't forced Shiloh to do anything. Not

really. She has asked Shiloh to wash her own bowl and to put the cereal back in the cupboard when she is through eating in the morning.

And she has asked Shiloh to sit down with her at lunch and dinner. *Together time*, she calls it, which makes Shiloh roll her eyes. She has asked Shiloh to help with the dishes after *together time*.

But the woman hasn't yelled or locked Shiloh in her room when she hasn't done these things.

"Want to come out to the barn with me?"

The woman has asked the same question. Every day.

"Want to come out to the barn with me?"

Three times a day. At least.

"Want to come out to the barn with me?"

And three times a day, at least, Shiloh gives the same answer.

"No, *thanks*."

The "*thanks*" is not to be polite.

The "*thanks*" is to let the woman know that she has no interest in going to the barn, that she'd never in a million years follow her to the barn.

Because Shiloh remembers, from the first afternoon, remembers the spooky dark of the barn, the whoosh of sound. Like somebody breathing, laughing.

No, Shiloh will not go to the barn. Even if the woman asks a hundred times a day, a thousand.

"Want to come to the barn with me?"

"No, *thanks*."

Shiloh stays in her room most of the time. A small room, but not bad. Except for how hot it is. No air-conditioning. Just a lousy fan.

At least the room is hers alone. She doesn't have to share with a bunch of other foster kids, like she has before, the older girls acting all mean and know-it-all, and the younger girls crying into their pillows every night.

The room is on the second floor, and the window is right above the kitchen door, so that when the woman comes out of the house in the morning, the tall, skinny red dog by her side, always, like a shadow, Shiloh can watch her.

Every morning Shiloh watches the woman and the red dog walk across the yard, the driveway, and disappear into the mouth of the barn.

Swallowed up. Ten minutes at least. Sometimes more. So that Shiloh starts to get jittery. Not about the woman. The jitters come from thinking about what to do if something happened.

The house is in the middle of nowhere. Shiloh doesn't even remember how they got here, which roads they took.

How would she explain to the ambulance people? If she had to call 911? Not that she wants to call 911. She never *wants* to call 911 again. Like a baby. Like a dumb baby.

But if she had to, if the crazy woman hurt herself in the barn with all those horses, what would Shiloh do?

So far she hasn't had to find out. The woman always appears again. Ten minutes. Sometimes twenty.

When the woman appears again, she's not alone. She's always leading a horse. First one and then another and another and another.

Four horses altogether. Besides the black one.

Grayish white. Dark brown. Medium brown with black legs. Tan and white.

One by one the woman leads the horses out of the barn and through the gate and into the field.

Not the field with the black horse. A different one.

All the fields around the barn are separated by wooden fences. Wooden fences with peeling white paint. Shabby, like everything else around here.

When the woman gets through the gate, she always releases the horses, one by one. And one by one they trot away from the woman, pushing their noses into the air, flicking their long tails. Circling, circling away.

But always circling back to the woman. That's what Shiloh doesn't understand. Why the horses come back if they don't have to.

After bringing out the horses one by one, the woman always disappears into the barn again. Longer this time. Twenty minutes at least. Thirty. After that she's always rolling a big wheelbarrow, loaded up with a mountain of brown.

Horse poop, probably.

And there's the reason. Right there. The reason the woman wants Shiloh to come to the barn. So she can shovel horse poop.

What a joke! There's no way Shiloh would shovel horse poop. Not in a million years. No way.

"What an idiot."

Inside the room Shiloh says it out loud. The way Slade would say it. Hard and fast, like spitting something gross out of your mouth.

Idiot! he'd say, and Shiloh's mom would have to agree with him quick or there'd be trouble.

Yeah, you're right, I'm an idiot.

Trying to say it fast enough, true enough, so that Slade wouldn't think she didn't believe him.

I don't know what I was thinking.

Laughing. A little. Laughing at herself.

Not at Slade. Never at Slade.

Because if Slade thought you were laughing at him, it was over.

Leave the thinking to me, Slade would say, grinning. *You're way too dumb to think for yourself.*

Grinning in that way that fooled you at first. Made you think that everything was okay. Made you believe he had changed his mind about hurting you after all.

"Idiot."

Shiloh's breath fogs up a patch of window.

"You're an idiot."

After the horse poop the woman comes out with the wheelbarrow again, this time with a little mountain of hay. She heads to the other field. The field with the black horse.

Shiloh can see the black horse from her window. Not that there's much to see.

The black horse just stays in one corner most of the time, staring at the fence. Moving only when the other horses or the woman—if anyone—comes close.

Then the black horse whirls around and rushes at the woman.

Rrrrhhhraaaa!

The same awful sound from the first day.

Rrrrhhhraaaa!

Only the gate stops him from running the woman down.

Rrrrhhhraaaa!

Shiloh doesn't get it.

Rrrrhhhraaaa!

Why the woman just stands there, without moving, without screaming back.

Rrrrhhhraaaa!

Why the woman doesn't use a whip or something. Isn't that what you use on a horse when it won't behave? Shiloh knows she's seen some old western on TV, a cowboy using a whip to let a mean horse know who's boss.

Shiloh would definitely use a whip.

But the woman just stands there. Talking or singing, it's hard to tell. Definitely her mouth is moving, though. And after a while the black horse finally shuts up and starts to eat.

Not that he wants to eat. Shiloh can tell. The black horse doesn't want to eat what the woman has brought him, but he can't help it.

Because he's starving. Shiloh understands now. All those bones sticking out. Like a skeleton. It's gross. She wonders why he's not dead already. She wonders if the woman just brought the black horse here to die, and if that's the reason, why she even bothered.

What happens to horses when they die, anyway? Do they go to heaven? Some big animal heaven? Will Shiloh go to heaven? She used to think so, when she was a little girl and her mom told her about heaven like it was a fairy tale so that it sounded like a perfect place except that you had to die to get there. Now that Shiloh is older, she definitely doesn't believe in fairy tales, and so she's not sure she believes in heaven, either.

•   •   •

JESSALYNN

The mare is in a hurry. She practically drags Jess from her stall to the turnout.

"Yep, he's still there," Jess says, releasing her girl, watching as she gallops to the black horse. Or at least as close as she can get.

Night will stay in quarantine in the far field for now, maybe forever. Because of the pneumonia, because of the meanness.

The mare trots along the fence line, tossing her head high in the air, shaking out her long white mane. Calling out a greeting.

Hmmmmmmmmmmmm!

She is ghostly white with a dusting of gray, like soot, sprinkled along her shoulders and back. A looker. But then Jess has always been a sucker for Arabians, ever since she was a little girl reading about the horses born straight out of the sands of the desert, half a world away.

Hhhmmmmmmm-mmmm!

Like all Arabians, the mare is small and dainty, but remarkably strong. And persistent. She keeps nickering across the divide, waiting for the proper reply.

Hhhhmmmmm-mmmmm!

Jess named her Persephone after rescuing her years ago. Persephone. A queen from ancient Greece, a "white-armed" goddess.

And like a goddess, Seph—as she's known now—expects the new horse to call back to her. Even though he is a stallion, she expects him to acknowledge her place as lead mare.

And acknowledge her he does.

Night explodes toward the fence, and Jess's old heart nearly stops.

Could the black horse actually clear the barrier? Even in his weakened state? Could he soar like a hawk zeroed in on its prey?

No. Of course not. He's not strong enough. Not yet. Maybe not ever again.

The black horse loses his balance near the fence line, stumbles, and, blaming Seph for this embarrassment, he starts screaming at the top of his lungs.

Rrrrhhhraaaa!

Seph takes a step back and brings her lovely head up to her full height. She endures the screaming, gazing back at the rude creature, ears flicking forward in surprise and alarm. Jess knows exactly what Seph would say if she could talk in human tongue.

Hey, what's your problem? I was just trying to say hello.

As it is, Seph stands her ground a moment more, and then snorts the air out of her nose, a bad smell. She turns abruptly, dancing away from Night. Tossing her silky gray mane. Picking up speed as she travels around and around the fence line, her whole body alert and prancing.

Showing off now. But Jess can't really blame her. The girl gave the boy a chance, but the stallion blew it.

With Seph happy and safe in the field, Jess heads to the barn for the rest of the crew. Staccato and Mercer Rex, the two geldings. And Ruby, the old bay mare.

Staccato always tries to imitate Seph, like an adoring younger brother. He dashes to the far fence to show he is not afraid of the black stallion. But when Night goes through the same routine, rushing and screaming, Staccato startles back as if he's touched electric wire. He trots away, falling in line behind Seph, turning to snort his disdain at the black horse from a safe distance.

Mercer Rex doesn't even give the new arrival a second glance. His only interest is the new tender grass that's shot up from the recent rains. He's the old man of the group. Solid. Unflappable. And Ruby sticks to Rex like the lifelong companion she's become.

This is Jess's family. Four horses and a dog. She loves them more than she can put into words. And she could stand here all day, watching them, but she has work to do. Always work to do.

Back inside the barn, the cats swirl about Jess's ankles. The swallows swoop through the high rafters on the way to their nests.

Jess flips on the old radio that's tied to a post. She likes to listen to NPR in the morning, and she doesn't mind when the classical starts playing after the voices have faded out.

It takes longer than usual. To muck out all the stalls, roll the manure inside the wheelbarrow out to the compost pile around back. Refill all the water buckets and the troughs of hay. All that mud wrestling at the rescue has taken its toll on her body. No doubt about it. She just doesn't bounce back the way she used to.

Jess calls to the horses as she goes in and out of the barn. She talks to Bella as she works.

Sometimes she catches a blur of movement at the second-floor window. A flutter of curtain. She thinks the girl is watching. She hopes so.

Space. That's what usually works. Giving the new foster kid a bit of space in the beginning. Something they're usually not used to.

And the horses, of course. Impossible for any kid to resist.

Although Jess has to admit, this one seems like a hard nut to crack. The social worker was right.

Tough as nails. Angry at the world.

With good reason. Probably. Although Jess doesn't know for sure. She's found, over the years, it's best not to know the details. She usually gets the picture soon enough.

Nightmares, outbursts, scars. Troubles have a way of showing themselves no matter how deep they're buried.

Jess does know that this girl will be her last. This time she will make sure to remove her name from the list. She's getting too old. For emergencies at four thirty in the morning. For angry kids.

The last one was a boy. More than a year ago. He was angry too, but ready. Ready to let the walls come down. He took to the horses right away. Especially to old Mercer Rex.

With Rex's help, the boy began to open up, began to laugh again. By the time he left Jess, he was ready to go to a real family. And Jess was proud. Like a grandma.

Jess would be a grandma if things had turned out differently. But she's not and they didn't and that's all she'll allow herself. She doesn't believe in self-pity. Never has.

The boy still writes letters to Jess. He writes letters to Mercer Rex as well. Letters Jess reads out loud to the old horse in the barn.

But the girl isn't ready. And there's hardly any time.

"A month, maybe two," Ms. Brown, the social worker, said. "We're trying to get everything squared away before school starts up again. We're waiting for a space to open at the RTC, the residential treatment center. That's her last stop, I'm afraid. But she's had chances all along. Good chances."

Jess wanted to say no. In fact, she tried. But Ms. Brown was surprisingly tough despite the sunny sweetness.

"We were really counting on you to help us out here," Ms. Brown said brightly. "We just don't have any other choice now, I'm afraid."

After the stalls are mucked and swept, Jess wanders out to the field again. Seph comes immediately, curving her long, graceful neck over the fence, nudging Jess gently with her velvet nose.

"Sorry, girl. Can't ride today. I'm still a little stiff."

Seph stretches out farther and wraps her neck around Jess's torso as if she is hugging her.

And Jess hugs her back.

Six

SHILOH

She has never lived anywhere that doesn't have a TV. Most places have had the TV on nonstop. Even the old couple watched the news all the time, though they kept the sound down.

"Sorry. I don't have a TV."

At first Shiloh thinks the woman is joking.

"Nope, no TV."

And then Shiloh thinks maybe it is a game.

If you can find the TV, you can watch it.

That's the kind of game Slade would play. Only he'd make sure you never found it. Or that it was broken when you did. And then he would laugh in a way that made you know how stupid you'd been to look in the first place.

"Haven't had a TV in years."

When Shiloh understands, when she finally understands

that the woman is not kidding about the TV, that she is not playing a game, she knows she has to break something.

Something special.

But what?

In the old couple's house it was easy to choose. The old lady had all these tiny glass figurines on a shelf in the living room. They made a tinkling sound when they hit the floor.

But here, in this house, it's hard to tell what is special. Everything looks old, used.

In fact, this house isn't so different from all the other houses Shiloh has lived in over the past few years. Shabby on the inside and out. Worn, mismatched furniture. Dog hair on the sofa and chairs. Newspapers and magazines stacked in the corners.

The TV, of course. That's what makes this place different. The no TV.

And the books. Everywhere. Floor to ceiling. Walls covered in books.

"Were you a librarian or something?"

The words come out one day at *together time*. Shiloh has tried to stay quiet. Tried to keep her mouth shut. But it's hard. Day after day. She forgets sometimes and blurts something out.

"What makes you ask that?"

The woman is slow. Maybe not as slow as the last one,

but definitely not the brightest bulb on the tree, as her mom used to say.

"Why do you have so many books, then? Did you steal them from the library?"

The woman takes a bite of food and chews about fifty times. Who needs to chew fifty times?

"I like books," she says at last. "Been collecting them for years. I have some you might like."

"Books are boring," Shiloh says. "Everything is boring here."

The woman takes another bite, and it's another million years before she speaks.

"There's always a lot to do in the barn."

Shiloh balls her hands into fists under the table. She could punch something.

"I'm not your slave." Spitting it out. Sticking her chin forward.

The woman is looking at her now. At least one eye is.

"Of course you're not my slave. I'd never treat you like a slave, Shiloh. Never. I just thought you might want to come out to the barn and meet my friends. Seph is very curious about you."

Shiloh keeps her fists in her lap. She tries, tries not to take the bait, like some dumb fish, but she can't help it.

"Who's Seph?"

"The Arabian. The grayish-white one."

"You mean Seph is just a horse?"

"A horse, yes."

"A dumb animal?"

"Well, Seph is far from dumb, I'll tell you that."

Shiloh snorts. "How do you know if that horse is dumb or not?"

"Because I've been around horses my whole life. Because I listen and I know. Horses aren't dumb at all. They each have their own personality, just like people do. But they're not dumb."

Shiloh stares down at her fists. The woman acts like such a know-it-all. She could punch her.

"If you have so many horses, why aren't you rich? Like those fancy horse farms in Lexington. Why do you live in such a dump?"

The woman gazes past Shiloh with the one eye. As if she is only just now seeing her kitchen.

"This place does need some fixing up, you're right about that." A little sigh. "I'm afraid I've been slowing down a bit, these last couple of years."

Shiloh doesn't understand why the woman doesn't react when she says something mean. Why her face doesn't crumple like the old lady's face always did toward the end.

"I'm not rich, but I have my own farm, my own house.

Those things are important to me. Not everybody with horses is rich. Not by a long shot. In fact, a lot of us are just getting by. Because it costs a lot to keep horses."

The woman is waiting. Like she expects Shiloh to have something to say to all that. As if Shiloh really cares.

"Anyway, Seph has let me know that she's curious about you. Horses can't talk, of course, but they do communicate."

"Com-mun-i-cate?" Shiloh repeats, pulling the fancy word apart like butterfly wings.

The woman just nods. She's so dumb she doesn't even know Shiloh is mocking her.

"I guess it's kind of like when you have a best friend, and you know what your best friend is thinking, even if they don't say a word out loud."

The woman is still smiling, and Shiloh can't look at her anymore. She needs to hit something.

The woman must know. She must know that Shiloh has never had a best friend. That she has never lived any place long enough.

"I guess you don't have any *real* friends." Shiloh lets the words do the hitting. "I guess you're just a lonely old lady."

"I do get lonely sometimes," the woman says, but she doesn't sound sad about it. "I guess everybody does now and then. I'm lucky to have Seph and Staccato and Mercer Rex and Ruby for company. And of course Bella here."

The woman reaches down to pat the dog at her feet—always at her feet. The dumb dog's long tail thumps against the wooden floor.

"But they're not people!" Shiloh spits it out. "They're just animals!"

"Animals make very good friends, actually."

Shiloh can't tell if the woman is looking at her. Not really. One eye is but one eye isn't.

"What happened to you, anyway?" Shiloh wants her words to be like fists, punching. "Did somebody beat you up?"

The woman cocks her head. She obviously doesn't get it.

"Your eyes. The way they're all weird." Shiloh makes a cross-eyed face. "The way one eye goes off in a different direction. Did somebody hit you and it made your eyes stuck like that?"

"No." The woman smiles again. She actually smiles. She's as bad as the state lady. "I was born this way."

"How do you see?"

"Well, I guess I could ask you the same thing."

"What? What do you mean? I see like a normal person."

"I don't really know what 'normal' means."

"'Normal' means like everybody else."

"Well, I think 'normal' is overrated. I think it's okay to be a little different."

For some reason, the way the woman says "a little different," Shiloh knows something has shifted. The woman isn't talking about herself anymore. She's talking about Shiloh. How she's different because she's a foster kid.

"I guess you don't have any real kids, either. Is that why you got me? Because you want to pretend you have a kid?"

Shiloh slams her fist down hard on the table. Her glass tips over. It doesn't break, but the milk spills along the tablecloth.

"Just like you pretend you have friends and they're only dumb horses?"

Shiloh can tell the woman is looking at her now. Even with the wacky eyes, Shiloh can tell. "Well, I have a real mom, not a pretend mom. And she wants me back. So don't think you can act like my mom. You probably don't know how, anyway."

Shiloh pushes up from the table, the chair tipping too. Upstairs she slams the door to her room as hard as she can.

The closet has a slanted ceiling that meets the wall just above her head. It's a perfect fit.

Shiloh pulls the pen out of her pocket, clicks it open.

Mrs. Lima Bean is stupid.

Mrs. Lima Bean is ugly.

Mrs. Lima Bean is a . . .

Shiloh writes a bad word, a really bad word. The word

Slade used to call her mom sometimes, the word she's heard some of the other foster freaks and their kids say. She still wants to break something that belongs to the woman—Mrs. Lima Bean—something special. But this is almost as good.

Mrs. Lima Bean will find the words one day, after Shiloh has left. Just like the old lady must have found the words by now in her own closet. Shiloh will be long gone, but she will have left her mark. Like a bruise or a scar across the skin. Something that might not last forever, but long enough.

NIGHT

The woman is not afraid of him, and this makes him angry. He has to keep reminding her, has to keep screaming and running her out. Because it's his field now. His domain. And he needs to protect it. Let her know she is the trespasser now.

The woman brings him food, but that makes no difference. He understands what bringing the food means. What is expected in return.

Gratitude. Servitude.

Because humans never give anything unless they expect to get something back in return.

He wishes he could refuse the hay and the oats, but he

can't. The hay is sweet and fresh. The oats in the bucket are warm. The water is cool and clear.

He can't remember the last time he had fresh hay, warm oats, clean water.

There's medicine inside the oats, of course. He can smell it. He knows it's there. He screams at her so she'll know that he knows. She cannot trick him. He tries to ignore the bucket and the hay for as long as he can, but he is too hungry.

And he does feel stronger. He knows the food is making him stronger. When he gets stronger he will be able to hurt the woman, kick at her, pin her to the fence, so that she will think twice. About coming into the field.

For now, though, he will eat when she brings him the food. He will wait till he is stronger.

So far, the woman has brought him food and water every morning and every night. Sometimes he wakes up and a blanket is over him, and the bucket is there.

But that's nothing to rely on. The food and the water. The woman is just trying to trick him. Trick him into trusting her. Bringing the food and water and hay every day so that he'll get used to that, so that he'll think she's nice, and he'll get soft.

And then stopping. Just like that. Stopping with the food and water. Disappearing for days, weeks.

Of course there is grass to eat here. He is in a field, not a stall. He is no longer locked away from anything to feed his empty belly except pieces of the old barn itself.

So he will not starve.

Still, he must be on guard at all times. He will never trust the woman, never trust a human. They talk in soft, soothing voices as they pull the bit tighter or snap the whip harder. As they wrap the chains around your neck.

No, that's not entirely true. The man with the chains was never soft and soothing. He never pretended to be one thing when he was really something else.

And in a way Night prefers that. He prefers it mean from the beginning. If that's the way it's going to be. Because then you know what to expect.

Night knew, from the beginning, about the man with the chains. He could tell right away. As soon as the man came near him. It was the smell. Night knew the smell. It always meant the same thing.

Meanness. Yelling and hitting, kicking.

Pain.

The smell is sweet but dangerous.

The woman doesn't have that smell. In fact she smells like horse. Other horses. The ones that sleep in the barn during the night, the ones that come to the fence, call to him, during the day.

The horses, especially the white mare, keep trying to get his attention. Sometimes he rushes at them, too, screaming, to let them know. He is not going to be their friend. But most of the time he ignores them. He has nothing to say.

JESSALYNN

Don't think you can act like my mom. You probably don't know how, anyway.

The girl's words. From earlier in the evening. Striking a chord.

Jess opens her eyes. Because she's not near falling asleep. Even though she's been trying for over an hour. Might as well give up the ghost, as her father used to say. She thinks about switching on the light, reaching for a book. Instead she stares up at the ceiling, at the crack she's spent a good part of her life studying.

Don't think you can act like my mom. You probably don't know how, anyway.

It's not like she hasn't heard those words before—or something like them—from the other foster kids.

I have a real mom.

You're not my family.

You're not my kin.

It's not like Jess has ever wanted to take the place of a child's real mother, a child's true family. That's not why she started doing this. Not at all.

Back then it just seemed like a natural extension of the riding lessons she was giving. She had the extra room; she had the horses. She liked the idea of providing a place where kids could come and stay, be around horses for a while, be safe.

I guess you don't have any real kids. Is that why you got me?

Jess was never looking to replace Maggie, her own daughter. She was never trying to get back what she had lost.

And yet. Here she is. Awake in the middle of the night. Staring at the ceiling. Mulling over the girl's words, wondering what she should do differently. Remembering.

A tree. A dragon. A lion.

That's what the crack in the ceiling above the bed could be, at different times, to Maggie's young eyes.

A bunny rabbit.

Especially after they'd first read *Madeline*, the story of the little girl living in the convent in France with all those other little girls and their beloved nun. In fact Maggie went through a stage of wishing she could live in such a place, lots of kids, beds all in a row. But she was an only child, and she eventually grew out of that stage, of wishing—and asking—for brothers and sisters that could never be.

74

Is that why you got me? Because you want to pretend you have a kid?

Right after the accident, Jess used to dream about Maggie every night. She used to dream about Rob. Sometimes together, sometimes separate, they would come and stand at the edges of a room, just out of reach. Jess couldn't see their faces, couldn't see any part of them really, but she could feel them. She knew they were there.

But that was years ago—so many years ago—and now there's a new dream. One that started up a few weeks ago.

A dream about a baby. Wrapped in a blanket, swaddled tight. So that Jess can touch the baby, hold it in her arms, feel its weight. But she can never see its face.

Strange, really. Jess hasn't thought about babies in years. But she doesn't mind the dream.

And she can't help but feel the tiniest bit hopeful, now, as her eyes begin to grow heavy at last, that the dream will be there in her sleep, waiting for her.

Seven

SHILOH

"Want to come to the barn?"

"No, *thanks*."

It's not that Shiloh hasn't been outside. She's walked outside, to the end of the driveway. She's counted the steps. She's watched the road beyond the fence to see how many cars go by.

Not many. It's like she and Mrs. Lima Bean are the only people left on Earth.

Today when Shiloh walks to the end of the driveway, she tries to see it inside her head. The streets they took to get here. She remembers going past the airport, but she can't remember the exit. She's never been outside Lexington much. Except to Tennessee sometimes. With her mom. To visit kin.

And down to Cumberland Falls. Once. Not long after her mom met Slade.

Back then Slade seemed nice, and her mom was so happy.

He took Shiloh and her mom—his ladies, he called them then—on a weekend trip. They stayed at a motel and ate a bucket of Lee's chicken on one of the big beds and watched cable TV. When it was dark, instead of going to sleep they drove out to the falls to see the moonbow. Like a rainbow, but with the moon instead.

Only a few moonbows in the world. That's what Slade said. Only a few places in the world where the light hits the water just right.

How old was she then? Four, five?

How old is the baby? A year maybe?

Shiloh closes her eyes and tries to see her sister—*she has a sister!* She sees a baby wrapped in a soft pink blanket. Bald maybe, the way Shiloh was, but with one of those cute pink headbands with the tiny bow on it.

Quiet. Sleeping.

That's how Shiloh tries to see her. Because if she cries. If she cries . . .

Shut up, you crybaby. Or I'll give you something to really cry about.

That's what Slade would say when Shiloh would start crying and couldn't stop. Slade hated crybabies.

Meet your sister. A screamer. Just like you.

Shiloh's eyes open, and the road goes sideways. The sky is in the wrong place. She is going to be sick. And so she turns and walks blindly away from the road, toward the trees. Squatting down beside the first one. Kneeling so that the knees of her jeans sink into dirt. Waiting, waiting for the cereal to come up and out.

But it doesn't, and after a while the sky goes back to being the sky.

And that's when she feels it. Somebody watching her. She lifts her head, opens her mouth, to shout at the woman to stop spying on her.

But it's not Mrs. Lima Bean. It's the black horse. Standing just behind the wooden fence. Head low. Face between the slats. Black eyes, like big glass balls, watching her.

"What are you looking at?" Shiloh says. She stands up. "What are you looking at?"

But the black horse doesn't say anything back. How could he? He's just a dumb animal.

Shiloh turns and stalks away.

NIGHT

He does not know why the woman has brought him here. What she wants.

Long ago when he was young and strong and fast, the reason why was clear.

To run. Fast. To be leader of the pack. To make the people watching stand up and yell so much their voices became a roar.

One owner and then another. All of them wanting the same thing. The terrible, beautiful roaring. The cape of roses. The winner's circle.

Why did it all stop?

Because he wasn't fast enough.

Because of the pain.

Barely there at first. A tenderness in one hoof. So that he could still win. He could still glide through the empty spaces between the other horses. He could still see where he had to go.

Open.

Close.

Open.

Close.

But then the tenderness became something else. A sharpness, like a pick jabbed under the skin.

One owner tried to make it right. He kept Night off the track. He put him in a nice stall so that he couldn't run, couldn't even walk on the one leg. So that he could heal.

And that worked. At first. Night felt good. He was ready to run, to win. But something had changed. Out there on the track. He couldn't see the way he had before. He couldn't slip through.

Open.

Close.

Open.

Close.

Close.

Close.

The man on his back didn't help. The many men. Because there wasn't just one after that. They were all different and all the same. As he got slower the men got meaner. Thinking the whip would make him faster, make him see what he couldn't anymore.

And then when he kept losing, it was a long drive to a new stable with less hay and oats. Day after day. Less. So that he grew weak and slower still.

The roaring was there. Inside him. But it was outside, too. For another horse. Not Dream of Night. Not anymore.

Again and again, a different stable. Less food and more horses, so that he had to fight for his share, and he began to lose track of where he was.

Until that long ride—the longest—to somewhere cold. Colder than he had ever been.

The pain got worse there, and the stiffness. Because

of the cold, without shelter, without enough food. So that he thought about not rising up from the snow. Some mornings. Never rising up. Because snow gets warmer when you don't move.

But then he *would* get up. And sometimes he would run. Like he used to. Run to stay warm. To stay alive.

And that's when the man came. The man with the chains.

He didn't have the chains at first. But he had the smell. From the beginning. The sweet smell.

The man brought him home again. Night could feel it. In his bones. The land he knew, the land of his birth. The same grass, same rolling hills, same dirt.

The man wanted what the others had wanted. For Night to be fast.

And Night tried. He tried. Because he wanted to run. It's what he was born to do.

But he was too weak, too lame. After all that time. Away from the other horses, the roaring. He was too slow.

And the man didn't like that. Didn't like that he had brought Night all the way home just to come in last.

And so the man would come to his stall at night. He would bring out the whip. And when Night kicked back and bit, when the blood flowed, the man brought out the chains.

"I'll show you," he'd say, his breath sweet and hard. "I'll show you who's boss."

And he would get the chains around Night's neck, even with the fighting and kicking. And he would pull the chains tighter and hook them to the wall. So that every time Night moved, the pain got worse.

The man would leave him that way and leave him that way. And when he finally came back, Night would be too weak to fight.

At least right off.

Once he had rested, it would start all over again.

The whip, the hitting, and finally the chains.

Longer and longer. Chained to the wall. No food and no drink.

Night nearly gave up again. Like when he had been in the snow. But then someone else came. Night isn't even sure. Just a blur. Human but a blur. The stranger unhooked the chain, left some food—stale feed and moldy hay, but it was food.

And it was the last. For a long time.

No one came. To feed him or to let him go.

And so he stayed inside the dark. Until it became a part of him. He stayed inside the dark. Until now.

•   •   •

JESSALYNN

A sound. Deep in the night.

The woman startles out of sleep, unsure at first what she's hearing.

The muffled, lonesome wail of a train? The whinny of a horse?

No. It's crying. Coming from down the hall. The girl is crying in her sleep.

Jess doesn't bother with the slippers or housecoat. She makes her way along the dark hallway, one hand to the wall to steady herself as she goes.

The door is closed, of course, and for a moment, Jess hesitates.

But there it is again. A kind of warbling cry. And so Jess takes hold of the knob and swings the door open.

The girl is sitting straight up in bed, her eyes wide and bright in the moonlight.

"No!" she cries. And then again, "No!"

"Shiloh," Jess says, gentle but firm, the way she'd talk to a spooked horse. "It's me, Jess. You're just having a bad dream is all. It's okay now. You're safe."

Still the girl doesn't move—she hardly blinks—and all at once Jess understands.

Shiloh's eyes are open, but she is still asleep, trapped inside her own head. Trapped inside her terrible dream.

"Shhh-shhhhh." Jess comes close. "Shhhhhh-shhhh." She kneels down, resting a hand on the mattress, not touching Shiloh, because she doesn't want to startle the girl awake. She needs to ease Shiloh back into sleep, ease her out of her nightmare.

"Oh, Shenandoah, I long to see you,

Away, you rolling river."

Soft and low, soothing, she hopes.

"Oh, Shenandoah, I long to see you,

Away, we're bound away, 'cross the wide Missoura."

Abruptly the whimpering stops. Shiloh cocks her head a little, as if she's listening.

And Jess prepares herself. For kicking, for fists, knees, and elbows. Because if the girl wakes up now and finds Jess here, beside her bed in the deep of night, she will surely lash out in fear, then anger.

But Shiloh's eyes flutter closed, and just like that she slumps back against the pillow, abruptly turning away from Jess, toward the wall, curling herself into a ball.

Jess waits to make sure. That the dream is gone, that the breathing is slow and steady. And then she pushes up, stiff in the knees, one foot tingly from holding still so long.

Back in her own room, she pulls on her jeans, under the gown, and finds a sweater. She won't be falling asleep any time soon, she can feel it. Might as well check on the black horse while she's up.

Eight

SHILOH

Sitting at dinner with Mrs. Lima Bean's lousy spaghetti. She's told the woman her cooking stinks. She's told her. But the woman just shrugs.

"Never been much of a cook, you're right about that."

So it's not even worth it.

"My granny tried her best. But I always wanted to be outside. With the horses. I never wanted to stay in a kitchen."

The woman wipes some spaghetti sauce off her mouth with a cloth napkin. Shiloh has never seen anybody use cloth napkins before.

"Or if I wasn't out with the horses, I'd be hiding in a tree, reading a book. I had a favorite tree I always went to. A big old laurel. I'd take a book and sit in that tree, and I could hear my granny calling for me, but I'd pretend I didn't hear, and I'd sit in the tree, reading till the sun came down."

"I bet your dad whipped you when you got home," Shiloh says. "For not listening."

"No." The woman shakes her head. "My father was a real gentle man."

"So your granny whipped you then."

"No. She'd make me go to bed without my supper sometimes. Or she'd make me stay inside extra long on a real pretty day and make me help her cook."

"What about your mom?"

"She died when I was a baby."

The woman probably thinks this will make Shiloh feel sorry for her. But it doesn't. Most of the people she's known don't have a mom. Or if they have one, the mom lives somewhere else.

"What a wimp! Both your dad and your granny. Wimps."

Shiloh scowls down at her lap. She doesn't climb trees. She's too old. But maybe she could find a tree around here, and then she'd hide all day and Mrs. Lima Bean would call and call and never know where she was. She wouldn't take a book, though. Who would want to read a book all day?

And that's when it hits Shiloh. An idea. How to get back at Mrs. Lima Bean for being stupid enough not to have a TV.

"So what books do you think I'd like, anyway?" she asks, trying to make her voice sound softer.

Mrs. Lima Bean's face opens up. Like it does when she is out in the field with the horses. It's more than a smile, it's like a door swinging wide. Shiloh almost feels sorry for her then. Almost.

"Well, let's see. How about I show you after dinner?" Mrs. Lima Bean says. "How's that?"

Shiloh nods, and she even makes herself smile a little. This will be easy. Easy as pie.

After they've cleared the dishes—Shiloh helps without just leaving this time—Mrs. Lima Bean gets up and goes to the shelf. The shelf packed with books. Floor to ceiling.

"This is one of my favorites."

Mrs. Lima Bean holds it out to Shiloh. It's not even a nice book. It has a ratty cover. And the picture on the cover is so old-fashioned, Shiloh wants to laugh. A drawing of a horse. All faded and boring.

"*Misty of Chincoteague.*" Mrs. Lima Bean reads the title.

And Shiloh can see. The way Mrs. Lima Bean is looking down at the book, the way she's holding it in her hands. It was the same with the old woman and her glass figures.

"My father read this to me at night when I was little, and later I read it to myself. Over and over again."

"Why would you read one book more than one time?" Shiloh scoffs.

"That's a good question."

The one eye is watching her, so Shiloh looks away.

"I guess it's because the story is familiar. Like an old blanket, or a warm, fuzzy sweater."

Here we go again. Shiloh can't help but roll her eyes. Books and horses for friends. What a loser. But she knows. She has to make herself seem interested. And she's good at pretending. When she wants to be.

"Have you always liked horses?"

The woman nods. She's still smiling.

"My father used to say that if you were able to look inside my head, it would be filled with tiny horses."

"That's dumb." Shiloh can't stop herself. "There's blood inside the head. Lots of blood. And when you fall and hit something, all that blood just spills right out."

She can feel the woman's one eye on her, so she doesn't look up.

"Would you like to read this?" Mrs. Lima Bean holds the book out. "You can take it up to your room if you like."

Shiloh almost feels sorry for Mrs. Lima Bean. Because this is so easy. But she takes the book anyway.

"Okay."

Back in her own room, Shiloh opens the book. She flips through the pages. There are pictures inside. Just like the cover. Old-fashioned, faded. Drawings of a girl and a boy and horses. An island. A boy racing on a horse. The pages are thin, and they make a crinkling sound when she turns them. They rip so easily, between her fingers, the way fairy wings would rip, maybe, if fairies were real.

nine

JESSALYNN

Brrrrnnnnnnng!

She is holding the baby in her arms when she hears the sound.

Brrrrnnnnnnng!

Is it crying? Is it the baby crying in the dream?

Brrrrnnnnnnng!

Is it the girl? Another nightmare?

Brrrrnnnnnnng!

No, it's the phone, ringing right next to her head.

"Hello?"

Grabbing it, blinking at the numbers on the clock. Too early. Even for Nita.

"Hello?"

Silence. On the other end. Open space.

Jess waits. She gives the caller one more chance.

"Hello, is anybody there? Do you have the wrong number?"

Click.

She returns the phone to the bedside table, listens a moment to make sure there's no other sound. And then slips back into sleep, into the dream.

SHILOH

Brrrrnnnnnnng!

Shiloh needs to find a place to hide.

Brrrrnnnnnnng!

But her sister won't stop crying and Shiloh is getting panicky.

Brrrrnnnnnnng!

She sets her sister—not a baby anymore but a tiny version of her mom—inside a drawer and slams it shut.

And then she starts looking for her own place to hide. But the other drawers won't open. No matter how hard she pulls.

Brrrrnnnnnnng!

And then she knows. It's not her sister crying. It's the phone. Down a long, dark hallway, unfamiliar, a place she's never been before.

She jerks up, eyes opening wide. She's on a bed, a bed she recognizes.

And then she's awake for real, listening.

Darkness all around. Silence.

No phone ringing.

She lies back down. The phone ringing—it was only a dream.

NIGHT

Brrrrrnnnnnnng!

"Watch this. I want you to see what he does when I ring this here little bell."

Brrrrnnnnnnng!

"Have you ever seen anything like that?"

Brrrrnnnnnnng!

"That boy is trained. Yessirreeee. Trained to run."

Brrrrnnnnnnng!

"One little bell. The starting bell at the race. That's what he was trained to hear. And that's all it takes to get this boy moving."

Brrrrnnnnnnng!

"Look at that!"

Hooves slamming against the boards of the stall. Because there's nowhere to go.

Brrrrnnnnnnng!

The black horse should have learned. But somehow he

couldn't. He couldn't stop his legs from moving. At the sound. Couldn't stop.

Brrrrnnnnnnng!

"Look at him trying to get somewhere!"

The man with the chains would come, and somehow he would make the sound. And every time, Night would try to kick through the door. At first he didn't understand why the gate didn't move.

Brrrrnnnnnnng!

And then he did know why, but he couldn't stop it.

Brrrrnnnnnnng!

And the man would laugh. And the men he was with would laugh. And Night would want to run and he would want to get at the man too.

Brrrrnnnnnnng!

The sound would go through his heart, and his legs would try to run.

Brrrrnnnnnnng!

But there were no empty spaces here, none at all. Only walls. Holding him in.

Ten

SHILOH

She thought the woman would ask about the book right away, but she hasn't. Shiloh keeps the ruined book by her bed, day after day. Most foster freaks would have found it by now, prying around in their sneaky way. They would have punished her.

Shiloh wants the woman to find it. It makes her mad that she doesn't even look.

"Want to come out to the barn?"

"No, *thanks*."

The same, day after day.

"Want to come out to the barn? It's nice and cool in there."

"No, *thanks*."

Today Shiloh sits on the porch to get out of the sun. She watches the woman go about her chores. Pushing the wheelbarrow full of horse poop around the corner, where she's making a giant pile. Shiloh doesn't want to know, but Mrs. Lima Bean tells her anyway.

"It's compost. Over time it mixes all together, and then it's good fertilizer."

"Fertilizer for what?"

"For the garden. For the vegetables."

"Don't tell me you put horse poop on your vegetables."

"Okay, I won't tell you."

Mrs. Lima Bean is grinning, and Shiloh just scowls.

"Well, I told you before, I'm not helping you with that stuff."

"It's okay. I'm used to doing it."

Shiloh clicks her tongue. She wishes the woman would ask her to do something so she could yell and scream and tell her how stupid she is. So the woman would have no choice but to grab her, hit her, even.

One of her foster homes—not the last one, but the one before—the man would spank her with a wooden spoon. The state lady wouldn't believe her. Because the guy would lie straight to her face.

"I would never raise a hand against any child," he would say.

So she ran away.

She'll run away from here. This will be easy. The woman locks the door at night, but just the front door. She doesn't lock Shiloh into her room.

And she's the only one. There isn't another kid to rat on her. There aren't any nosy neighbors.

It's perfect.

Except for how far out it is.

Should she follow the highway? State troopers are always on the highway. And you're not supposed to walk along it anyway.

But she doesn't know any other roads back to Lexington.

And so tonight, at *together time,* she asks Mrs. Lima Bean, "Do you have any books about Kentucky?"

Mrs. Lima Bean looks so happy. The same when Shiloh acted like she cared about what her favorite book was.

"Let's see, this one's pretty good."

"Does it have any maps?"

"No, I don't think so. Just photographs."

"Do you have one that shows where we are?"

The one eye is looking at her. Shiloh is sure the woman can read her thoughts.

"I've never been this far from Lexington before. I wanted to see where we are. Learn something about this area."

It's so fake, Shiloh is sure the woman will see right through it. But she doesn't.

"Hmmm." Mrs. Lima Bean pulls out another book. "Here's one."

She's so dumb she'd fall for anything. That's what happens when you have only horses and dogs for friends.

So Shiloh studies the book that night. She's only about thirty miles from Lexington. As the crow flies. But it will take a long time to walk. A lot longer than it took to drive. There's a smaller road on the map, one that skirts the highway.

That's what she'll do. Follow the smaller road.

But how will she find her mom? Once she gets to Lexington?

She remembers the last phone call on her birthday, at the old couple's house. She wishes there was a way to trace a phone call, like they do in spy movies. She knows her mom doesn't live in the old apartment. But Shiloh will go there anyway. Maybe the neighbors will know.

Shiloh rips the map from the book.

Now that she knows the way, all she has to do is get ready.

It will be as easy as one, two, three.

JESSALYNN

A sound close by.

Is it the phone again? Another wrong number in the middle of the night?

The woman sits up and listens.

No, not the phone. The girl.

Jess is out of bed and down the hallway in no time.

Inside the room, the girl's eyes are wide open in the dark, like usual.

"Shiloh, it's me. I'm coming into your room now. You're having a nightmare."

Jess makes the same announcement each time. So that the girl will know, if she starts to wake. So she'll under-stand. Jess isn't coming into the darkened room to harm her.

"Shiloh, it's okay. You're safe."

Jess uses the same word, night after night. *Safe.* But she has started to wonder: Is it only a word—*safe*? Will Shiloh ever truly know what it means to be safe?

"Oh, Shenandoah, I long to see you.

Away, you rolling river."

Jess sits down on the edge of the bed.

"Oh, Shenandoah, I long to hear you."

Gently she reaches out and takes Shiloh in her arms.

"Away, we're bound away . . ."

The whimpering stops. The girl's body goes rigid at first, and then relaxes a little, and a little more, so that Jess is cradling Shiloh.

"'Cross the wide Missoura."

Jess keeps humming the tune after the words have run

out, rocking gently, watching Shiloh's face in the moon-light.

Without the deep scowl. Without the flashing eyes.

Not so different from Maggie at this age. Now that Jess has a chance to see, without the guard going up.

Shiloh has the same fair hair as Maggie. The same dusting of freckles across the bridge of the nose. The same long, coltish face and slender body, thin shoulders tucked like bird wings under the faded nightshirt.

Not so different.

Maggie had nightmares, too, around this age. But of course hers were the usual kind. Something scary from TV or the movies, a tragedy on the news. Nothing in Maggie's life to cause the kind of fear Jess sees when she enters this room now, in the dead of the night.

The girl stirs; she lets out a whimper. But she doesn't wake. And Jess begins to ease her back down onto the pillow, trying to untangle herself without jostling the girl out of her peaceful sleep.

And that's when Jess feels it. A small patch of roughness, where the nightshirt has pulled sideways over one shoulder.

Jess takes a deep breath, steels herself against what she might find.

Five. No, six little circles. Jess sees them now. Clustered close together. The skin raised, hard and circular, scarred.

Jess closes her eyes. She knows. She should be used to this by now. She's seen burn marks before. Cigarette burns.

But she's not. Used to it. And her hands are shaking from anger, from disbelief, as she eases the nightshirt back in place, tucks the sheet around the girl's thin shoulders, leaves the room.

Who could do such a thing to a child? Hold a cigarette— a lit cigarette—against the skin? Not once, not twice, but *six times*?

Jess doesn't bother getting dressed. She slips on her boots and walks out to the barn in her nightgown. She heads right to Seph's stall. And Seph is there, waiting for her, like always. And Jess presses her cheek against Seph's warm neck and does not move and does not say a word. Because she doesn't have to.

Eleven

SHILOH

The black horse looks dead. Lying still in the corner of the field, a pile of bones and skin. A heap of nothing.

Maybe he died overnight and Mrs. Lima Bean hasn't noticed yet.

Shiloh glances back toward the barn. The woman is still in there. The girl clicks her tongue, angry suddenly, that the black horse is dead and the woman is clueless.

Shiloh inches closer, stops. She watches the space right above the horse's chest. To see if it will rise again.

It's what she used to do, with her mom. After all the screaming and yelling was done and Slade had slammed out the door.

She'd be too afraid to move yet, but she'd peek out. She'd watch her mom's body lying on the floor. She'd watch, and wait. Make sure her mom was still breathing.

The last time, the very last time, she couldn't tell. And

blood was coming out of her mom's head. A lot of blood. And so she panicked. Like a dumb baby. Panicked and called 911.

She would never panic like that now. Never.

And she doesn't care if the black horse lives or dies. Not really. She's just curious.

"Hey, you," she whispers so no one could possibly hear. "Hey, you." The black horse seems to vibrate. His legs jerk forward and his body rises up, straight up, from the ground.

The girl freezes in her tracks. Scared, but ready.

If the black horse rushes at her the way he rushes at Mrs. Lima Bean, if he screams at her, she's ready. She'll scream right back.

But the black horse doesn't move, he doesn't scream. He just stands there. Watching her.

"I thought you were dead."

The words pop out; the horse doesn't move.

"You sure looked dead."

Except for the ears. The horse's ears are moving. Fanning forward, and back again.

"What's the matter with you, anyway?"

Shiloh waits, although she's not sure what she's waiting for.

"Are you sick?"

Forward and back. Just the ears. Nothing else.

"You don't look right."

The big head dips down. The horse lets out a loud snort, and Shiloh startles back, she can't help it.

She wants to leave, but for some reason she just stands there.

"I hate it here," she says after a while. "Just like you."

The head bobs up. The eyes are all black today. No white. No red.

"I'm going to run away. My mom is waiting for me. And I have a baby sister. I've never seen her before. I don't even know her name. My mom forgot to tell me. But they're waiting for me. My mom and my sister. So I'm going to run away."

The black horse turns now. His whole body. Away from her.

And all at once Shiloh realizes what she's doing. Talking to a horse. Just like Mrs. Lima Bean.

Crazy.

The craziness is rubbing off.

The girl whirls around. She flies back to the house. Without saying another word.

•   •   •

nIGHT

He does not know what she wants. The child. He does not know anything about human children. Except that they are small and defenseless. No hooves. No hair to speak of. At least not on their bodies. Tiny mouths and teeth.

He does not know why she stands there sometimes, watching him. Speaking words to him. He does not know why he doesn't warn her, doesn't chase her away.

Twelve

JESSALYNN

Jess has decided to try something new. She rides Seph right up to the porch, where the girl is sitting, her legs dangling over the edge.

The girl is surprised, scared even. Although she's trying hard to hide it. She scoots backward, a crab scuttling, as fast as she can along the wooden floor. So Jess eases Seph back as well.

"What are you doing?"

Eyes flashing up at her, the familiar scowl after the surprise.

"I told you Seph wanted to meet you."

The girl is about to say something smart, turn away, Jess can tell, but she also knows this: Seph is hard to resist. Especially up close. The big, dark eyes fringed with long lashes. The gorgeous face. The mouth, curving upward, as if smiling.

"What kind of name is Seph?"

The girl spits it out.

"Seph is short for Persephone. In old Greek myths, Perse-phone was a goddess of the underworld, a goddess of rebirth."

"So?"

"So I think it fits her pretty well. When I found her, she was so thin, I didn't think she was going to make it. But she did. She healed so quickly, it was like she had been born again."

Hands curled into fists. Always ready for a fight.

"What do you mean, when you *found* her?"

"When I rescued her. That's what I do. I help rescue horses."

"From what? What do horses need rescuing from?"

"From people who don't look after them properly. From bad situations."

The girl doesn't say anything for a while, but she is thinking. Jess can see the wheels turning. And she is moving closer. One millimeter at a time.

And Seph is waiting. Such a patient horse. So intuitive. Seph knows not to make any sudden movements or the girl will fly.

Fight or flight. The way a horse is wired. Either to kick out at what they don't understand, or to run from it. Over the years Jess has come to find that humans aren't wired so differently.

"Seph doesn't bite," Jess says in a quiet voice.

The click of the tongue, the roll of the eyes, both so familiar to Jess now.

"I'm not afraid. I'm not afraid of some dumb horse."

"I didn't think you were. I just wanted you to know." Jess pauses. "Some horses do bite. You have to be careful if you don't know a horse and their habits. But Seph isn't a biter."

Inching closer.

"I found Seph in a pen with a lot of other horses. There wasn't enough food, and so she was skinny because she'd had to fight for her share. She had a lot of bites and scratches from the other horses."

Jess keeps talking. The girl's fists begin to release. Slowly, so slowly you would miss it if you weren't sitting on top of the horse, Seph is stretching herself out toward the girl. Waiting, waiting for the girl to make contact.

"Seph is part Arabian. That's one of the oldest breeds in the world, one of the noblest. They originally come from Arabia. Every single one throughout the world can be traced back to those first horses, born in the desert. Even Seph here."

One hand reaches out, fingers fluttering along the horse's jaw. Making contact. Pulling away. Reaching out again. Touch.

"You can always tell an Arabian from other horses. They're small and graceful. Dainty. But they're strong for their size, quick, light on their feet. And very smart."

Jess keeps talking so that the girl can touch the horse again. She can see something shifting. Ever so slightly. Shifting.

"What's the black horse's name?"

This time it's Jess's turn to be surprised.

"Oh, I've never told you his name?"

The girl doesn't answer, but her silence always manages to say a lot.

"Dream of Night."

The girl pulls her hand away from Seph. She scowls toward the far field.

"That's his full name," Jess continues. "Thoroughbreds always have a full name that they're registered under, a professional name they race under. But lots of times owners will shorten it. I've just been calling him Night."

"He hates you, doesn't he?"

So different in the light of day. This girl. Nothing like Maggie now. So tough and hard. Like the skin on her shoulder. The scars rough and ugly, covering the hurt place.

"Well, he's real angry, that's for sure," Jess answers.

"He won't let you near him."

"He's scared to let anyone near him."

Fists again.

"He's not *scared* of anything."

The girl's face is flushed. She whirls around and slams back into the house.

And Jess knows. She's discovered something. She can't believe she didn't see it before.

night

Night Warrior was the sire. Dream's Delight was the dam.

The blood running strong and true in his veins. Blood meaning everything to a Thoroughbred. The line of champions going back through time.

Warrior's Revenge.

Warrior's Sun.

Warrior's Promise.

Winners all. On the sire's side.

And on the dam's side, as well, of course. Dream's Delight, a mother to the best of the best.

Mother.

What does he remember of being a foal?

Almost nothing.

Except.

The fortress of her body when he knew nothing of the

world beyond. The nudging, gentle but firm, to rise up on his own four legs, to run.

And he wanted to run. He wanted to run faster than every other colt in the field. He wanted to run faster than the wind.

And so he did not look back when the men came for him and put him inside the rolling metal box that very first time. He did not turn his head even though he could hear her voice amid all the other voices, all the other mares calling to their young.

Eeeeeee!

He knew he would never see her again.

Eeeeeee!

And he was scared. For the first time in his life. He was scared. But he did not look back.

SHILOH

"Dream of Night."

She says it out loud, and the black horse raises his head from the ground.

"That's your name."

The black horse blasts air out his nose. A dragon breathing fire. A monster. He definitely still looks like a monster.

She will scream back if he tries to scream at her.

"Dream of Night." She says it again, and then, "Not bad."

The name is perfect, really. The black horse is like the night, dark and scary. Like dreams, too. Shiloh had a dream last night. A dream she's had before. Many times.

In the dream Shiloh is playing hide and seek, and at first she thinks it's her mom who's doing the seeking, but then it's Slade. She never actually sees him. But she knows he's there. She can feel him behind her, bigger than in real life, and she keeps opening doors, but the doors never go anywhere. The doors don't lead into the closet like they're supposed to. They don't lead into the basement or even out to the street. But she keeps opening the doors anyway, like a dummy, and then she hears the laughter, and she knows Slade is laughing at her because she keeps trying to get away and she can't.

"My name is Shiloh."

She waits. The black horse hasn't looked away.

"It's a battlefield. Down in Tennessee. A Civil War battlefield. A lot of people died there. It's where my mom is from. And she always thought when she'd have a girl she'd name her Shiloh Grace."

The black horse looks off to one side, but then his head swings back again.

"I don't know my sister's name. Mom forgot to tell me."

Shiloh glances toward the barn. No sign of Mrs. Lima
Bean.

"Maybe when I run away, I'll open the gate."

She takes a step forward, but the black horse doesn't bolt.

"I'll open the gate, and you can run away too."

Thirteen

JESSALYNN

Together time, and the girl is listening. Even though she's acting like she's not. Pushing the food around on her plate with a fork, head down, but listening, Jess can tell.

"Dream of Night is a Thoroughbred. He was bred for racing."

Like a story, the stories her father used to tell about legendary horses before bedtime. Pegasus, the winged horse, who carried Greek gods on his back. The Black Stallion, whose adventures took him to faraway shores. Maybe she should have started with *Once upon a time*, but she knows the girl would have clicked her tongue, rolled her eyes at that.

"Thoroughbreds can be temperamental. And when they race, they aren't trained to be sweet and easygoing. They're trained to be fierce and strong, and to run. Very, very fast."

The girl isn't eating, even though it's one of her favorites, or at least something she doesn't say is so "lousy." Mac and cheese casserole, not from a box. Made from scratch. The way Jess's granny used to make it. One of the only granny recipes Jess ever truly mastered.

"Dream of Night won his first race, and then he won another. He kept on winning for a while. Until something happened."

The girl glances up then. A hint of interest. Not wanting to show it, though.

"A tiny fracture in his front right pastern, I'll bet. I doubt the owners noticed it at first. They might not have noticed until he started slowing down, started losing the race. Maybe the first owners sold him because they couldn't afford to keep a horse that didn't win, maybe the next owners didn't know he was injured—"

"Why do you keep saying 'maybe'?" The girl is scowling. "Don't you *know*?"

Jess shakes her head. "When you rescue a horse like Night, there's a certain amount of information that's known for sure, because he's registered, which means there's a record of his races. But once he stops racing, he can drop out of sight, and you just have to guess what his life might have been like all those years he wasn't racing. But you can never really know for sure."

"It would help if he could *talk*, right?"

Jess sees the smirk, knows the girl is trying to catch her out on the whole horse-communicating thing. And so she nods and grins to show she's in on the joke.

"Night tells me a lot without actually speaking."

"You mean when he's screaming at you?"

Jess chuckles. The girl is certainly quick. "Actually he tells me things without ever saying a word."

Shiloh clicks her tongue, but she can't resist. "Like what?"

Jess takes a deep breath. Where to begin?

"Like how he's been starved nearly to death."

"That's easy to see," Shiloh scoffs. "I don't know anything about horses, but I know that. He's a skeleton."

"Night's probably two hundred pounds less than a horse that size should be. That tells me that his last owner didn't care enough to give him food or water."

"Maybe the owner just couldn't afford to feed him. He didn't have the money, and it wasn't his fault."

Jess senses something beneath the words. "Could be. But a horse is a big responsibility. If the owner couldn't afford to feed him, he should have tried to find another home for him. He should have sold him or given him up for adoption. Before things got so bad. He shouldn't have just let him starve."

The girl shrugs like she doesn't care.

"Night's nearly bald and he's covered with sores," Jess

continues. "That tells me that his owner didn't care enough to keep his coat clean and healthy."

More silence.

"His knees are swollen up real bad, and he's stiff, and lame in those front legs. That tells me he was worked pretty hard, made to race through the pain, never given a chance to heal. The right way."

Shiloh has put down her fork. Both hands are in her lap, clenched into fists probably, although Jess can't see.

"The anger." Jess needs to tread lightly now. "The anger tells me that he doesn't trust humans because he doesn't have any reason to. He's never met a human he could trust. All the humans in his life have hurt him."

Shiloh is staring down into her lap now. Jess isn't sure she should keep going.

"The scars tell me that somebody was mean to Night. Really mean."

Jess can feel it. The way the girl's body has gone rigid. Every muscle tensed, waiting. Like a horse when it senses danger. The moment before flight.

"The scars tell me that the person who was supposed to take care of Night, who was supposed to love him and keep him from harm, didn't do that. They hurt him instead."

Shiloh explodes up from the table. Muscles in motion now. Body flying for the doorway.

"Shiloh—," Jess begins, but the girl's footsteps are already pounding the stairs. The bedroom door slams overhead.

Jess lets out a sigh. She reaches down below the table, to stroke the place between Bella's ears.

We'll take it slow.

Words she said to the girl on that first day. When there was more time.

SHILOH

The woman still hasn't asked about the book. Shiloh has ripped out half the pages, stuffing them under her mattress.

Tonight, though, she pauses before she rips. She looks at the drawing of the boy riding a horse, laughing, smiling. Happy.

She wonders what it feels like to ride a horse, wonders if it feels like flying.

Fourteen

JESSALYNN

"Hello?"

The phone again. Jostling her out of sleep. Nearly the same time, when Jess looks at the clock.

"I think you must be dialing the wrong number." Jess recites the number and waits. She wants to be helpful. But there's only silence on the other end. Some breathing maybe. Not heavy breathing. Even so, it must be kids playing a trick. Prank phone calls.

But why her?

A random name out of the phone book, probably. A decision to keep it up every night. Well, not every night. Has it been? Jess has lost track. Every other night.

"Stop calling, now," Jess says in a firm voice. "Please." She clicks off, examines the phone a moment.

Should she unplug it? Turn off the ringer?

No, she can't do that. What if there really was an emergency?

Bella has lifted her head. Her dark eyes are watching Jess, brow furrowed, as if she's considering the options too.

"Go back to sleep," Jess says, rubbing a hand along the dog's neck.

Bella thumps her tail once against the covers, sighs, rolls onto her side.

Jess lies still for a while, then she gets up, feet finding slippers. She walks quietly down the hall, listening to make sure the girl is peaceful. And then she heads downstairs to check on the horses.

SHILOH

She doesn't always know where she is when she wakes up. Not at first. There have been so many apartments, houses, rooms. All of them merging together when she first comes out of sleep.

She opens her eyes now, and she hears the fan burring near her head. She hears the pots and pans, muffled, from just below. A murmur of voices. No, one voice. The woman is talking to the dog. No one else listening.

When she hears the screen door creak open and snap shut, Shiloh gets out of bed. She looks out the window. The woman is walking to the barn, the dog following close behind.

Shiloh lets her eyes run along the fence line to the black horse.

He's up already. Staring at the corner of the fence, like he does for most of the day, like a dummy.

What does she care if he has scars? What does it matter to her?

He's a mean horse. He probably got what he deserved. He probably kicked and bit somebody, screamed at them. And they weren't as dumb as Mrs. Lima Bean. They kicked back.

Shiloh turns away from the window. She heads to the closet.

She should be packing her bag already, getting ready to go. For some reason she's stopped thinking about running away. But she needs to get her head straight. That's what her mom said. The last time she saw her.

I need to get my head straight.

Shiloh didn't know what her mom meant then, but she knows now. Shiloh needs to stop talking to horses and get her head straight about leaving. Before it gets too late and the state lady comes for her and drags her away to someplace else. The RTC. Where they lock the doors from the outside and have guards snooping around all the time. This place is easy.

Easy to leave.

Shiloh tugs at the suitcase. She yanks the few shirts from

the hangers, stuffs them inside. She stops only to admire the work she's done on the wall. A whole column of words. From floor to ceiling. She wishes she could see Mrs. Lima Bean's face when she finds it.

Shiloh takes the pen from the shelf, clicks it open. She wants to add something, but she can't think of a new word, so she starts drawing instead.

She knows she's not any good at drawing, but she does it anyway. And when she's through, she leans back to see.

Her drawing doesn't look like the real thing. But she shades in the black between the lines.

Dream of Night.

She writes the name underneath. She wants to write something about the black horse, how he's mean and ugly and stupid. But she doesn't. She runs a finger along his back, as if she is touching him. As if she could.

NIGHT

Something heavy weighing him down. The blanket again. He shakes it off and rises to his feet.

The blanket smells like the woman. He snorts at it, pressing it into the ground, ripping at it with his teeth, stamping it with his hooves.

He needs to keep watch. Not just during the day. He knows the woman is trying to trick him. Putting the blanket over him while he sleeps. Leaving the warm bran mash for him to find.

Maybe the human child is trying to trick him too.

During the day Night leaves his corner to rush at the other horses sniffing and meddling at the fence. He screams at the woman when she comes out of the house. He will scream at the human child when she comes too close.

He trots along the fence line. One lap, two. He is free. He is flying.

And then.

Something always pulls him back, jerks him back to his corner.

Is it the pain?

No. Not the pain. Something else. Something just as strong.

It pulls him back to the corner of the field. To the fence.

He screams at the fence. He kicks at it, but it doesn't fall away.

Planks of wood, joined together. That's all a fence is. Nothing more. He has known fences his entire life. Some have been able to hold him, and some have not.

Back when he was young, he could sail over a fence if he felt like it. He could find ways to lift the boards, and step through. Once, there was a filly who would work at a chain until it fell from the gate, and they would thrum through the opening together and down to the creek. They would splash and chase the birds flying up from the ground. The grass was always sweetest there.

But he is changed. He knows this. The chains did not change him, but the darkness did. The solitude.

The field is his. He will fight for every inch of it. He will kick and bite at anyone who thinks they can come into his territory and challenge what is his.

But the corner pulls him back, harder than any chain. And he must spend part of the day staring at the walls of his prison.

The girl doesn't come all morning, and he doesn't care. He's glad. The woman gives him food and he screams at her. He goes back to his corner.

Asleep on his feet. Waking and sleeping the same sometimes. Unsure which is the memory, which is the real thing.

Later, when the sun is overhead, he looks up and the girl is there. Just beyond the fence.

He is going to rush at her, scream at the top of his lungs. But he doesn't. And he doesn't know why.

Fifteen

JESSALYNN

Jess is in the barn when she hears a truck pull into the driveway. She knows it's Nita by the sound of the engine.

"Hey, girl, came to check on you," Nita calls.

"Howdy, stranger." Jess shades her eyes as she comes out into sunlight.

"I know, I know, but I ended up taking a couple more besides the palomino, so I've been busy."

"Tell me about it."

Jess glances toward the back field. She knows Shiloh was out there with the black horse. The girl must have ducked behind a tree when Nita drove up.

"Hey, he's looking better," Nita says, following Jess's gaze.

Jess can hear the surprise in her voice. She watches Nita stride toward the gate.

Rrrrhhhraaaa!

The black horse whips around and rushes at Nita, screaming. Nita stops and waits.

Rrrrhhhraaaa!

"Hasn't lost any of his charm, has he?" Nita calls over her shoulder.

Rrrrhhhraaaa!

The black horse lets out one last scream and turns away from Nita, heading back to his corner.

"He's filling out, though," Nita says. "Lungs sound better too. Guess he's got a ways to go on his manners, though, huh?"

"You can say that again." Jess lets out a laugh. "Still can't get near him. Except when he's asleep."

"I bet he'll come around soon enough. You always get 'em to come around. Look at Seph there. You brought her back from the dead."

"Seph was different, and that was a long time ago. I was a lot younger."

"Oh, come on, you're not old. You were holding your own with all those wild horses last month."

"Yeah, and I paid for it too." Jess gives a nod toward the house. "Want some coffee?"

"Sure."

The two women head for the kitchen. Inside, Jess gets the coffeepot going while Nita leans against the counter, getting her up to speed on the rescue situation.

"The owner is making a big stink all over town. He wants them back. Can you believe it? Says he's taking it to court."

"I'm not surprised," Jess answers. "But he may just be fighting it for show."

"He's not from around here," Nita continues. "Had some big ideas about being a horseman, apparently. Bought that place for a song two years ago, and started buying up horses at auctions. Tried to race some, but never won anything. A drunk. That's what people say. Couldn't keep anybody working for him. Neighbors hadn't seen him in a while. It was a neighbor that turned him in, Tom said."

Jess glances out the window as she gets the mugs down from the cabinet. The girl has reappeared, standing in her usual place across the fence from the black horse.

"He's been showing up at the Humane Society, two sheets to the wind and threatening everybody," Nita continues.

"Just blowing off steam, I guess," Jess says.

When the coffee is ready, she pours out two mugs, black, and goes to sit at the table.

"Maybe you're right," Nita says, leaning against the counter. "But I'm glad he doesn't know where we live. Sounds like a nut. And there's no way I'm handing my horses back to some drunk. I'll go to jail first."

Jess watches her friend's face. Nita is like the foals they

rescued the other day. Still feisty and full of fire. She is younger than Jess by about fifteen years.

"That would do your horses a lot of good," Jess says. "You in jail."

"I'm not giving 'em back! No way!" Nita's eyes are wide with indignation. "What about him?" She throws a thumb over her shoulder. "Can you imagine giving that fella back, after all he's been through?"

Jess takes a sip of coffee. She remembers when she was a little girl, and her father would sell the foals they'd birthed and gentled. It broke her heart every time. But she knew deep down her father was right. It was part of life. Knowing when to let go.

"Hey, who's that?" Nita has turned toward the window. "Who's that girl out there? You giving riding lessons again?"

"No. That's my new foster kid."

"You didn't tell me you were doing that anymore. Thought you'd stopped."

"Thought so too."

"How's it going?"

Jess lets out a sigh. "Slow."

Nita is still watching out the window. "Hey, I thought you couldn't get near that horse."

"Not when he's awake."

"Well, then, you might want to see this."

Jess pushes up from the table and goes to stand next to Nita. What she sees takes her breath clear away.

Shiloh is standing at the far fence. Closer than she's ever been. And she is reaching through the slats, holding her hand out toward the black horse. And the black horse just stands where he is, without startling or screaming or moving at all. He just stands there, and the girl's hand reaches out and she touches him.

Shiloh touches Night.

SHILOH

She has a secret. She has touched the black horse.

The black horse hasn't let anybody touch him. Mrs. Lima Bean has tried. But only Shiloh has done it.

She can't explain how it happened. But somehow she knew.

She hid when she heard the wheels on the gravel. She thought it might be the state lady, coming to check on her. But it was a truck. A tall woman wearing a cowboy hat, with a long dark braid hanging down her back. A friend of Mrs. Lima Bean's.

Shiloh waited until Mrs. Lima Bean and the woman

went into the house. She waited, and when they stayed inside, she came out from behind a tree.

The black horse was so close. She wanted to touch him. She didn't know why. She wanted to feel what it was like.

It wasn't like she'd expected. He wasn't soft, velvety, like the white horse. He was rough. His skin along his shoulder rippled when she touched him, but he didn't move away. He stood there, and at first he didn't even look at her. He acted like he didn't know she was touching him. And then he moved. And his mouth came closer and she was sure he was going to chomp down on her fingers. But he didn't. He blew hard, through his nostrils. Some snot flew out, and Shiloh almost pulled away. It was gross. But she didn't do that either. And then he looked at her.

It was the first time he had turned to look at her. And he was like Mrs. Lima Bean in a way, because one eye was looking at her but one eye was on the other side of his head, so he definitely couldn't see her with both eyes.

Shiloh looked into that one eye, and what she saw was herself. Like a mirror, almost. Like a trick mirror at a fun house, making you look different than you really are, but the same, too.

Shiloh peered into that one eye, and her face got bigger and bigger and bigger until it disappeared. And all she could see was black. And then she pulled back and saw herself again, her whole self. Even the hand reaching out.

And she wondered what the black horse was seeing. If he was seeing himself in her eyes too.

NIGHT

Touch.

A slap. A punch. A kick.

Before that. What came before that?

The first bridle. A fight he nearly won. But didn't. And then the saddle. A man tucked on his back.

Even after he had learned what he needed to know to run, to be fast, to be leader of the pack, he would still try to get them off, those men.

A tree, a fence, a sudden stop.

Tricks he learned to free himself. For a little while. Not long enough.

Men are clever. Eventually they find ways to hold on.

Nightmare.

Something he was called in the first place too. By the grooms who came to care for him.

Nightmare.

Because he did not make their job easy.

A bite. A kick. A swing of the head.

It's not that he did not want a clean coat, a good scratching, hands massaging sore muscles. He wanted those things. But he also wanted them to know. Who he was. Who they were dealing with.

Dream of Night.

Son of champions.

Leader of the pack.

Who is he now?

The certainty is gone. Like the roaring of the crowd. The knowledge comes and goes, the memories of greatness.

Touch.

He does not know why he let her do it. The child. He has not let anyone touch him for a long time.

The man with the chains would come, and Night would fight and fight and fight. So that only with the metal around his neck, with the darkness crushing in, could he be touched.

The men who brought him from the barn. They touched him, yes, but he kicked and bit and butted so that they would know not to do it again.

The woman wants to touch him, and he will not let her.

But the child, the human child.

She held out her hand, and he does not know why he did not warn her, did not sink his teeth into her flesh to make her pull the hand away.

Maybe it's because he knows this child, even though he has never seen her before this place.

The fear and anger and pain.

He knows. Her.

And so he did not warn or bite or scream, and the hand reached out, small and trembling like a leaf in the wind, and he let the hand touch his mouth, his cheek. He let it stay.

Part two:
Trust

One

SHILOH

She's not doing it for the woman. She's doing it for the black horse.

Mornings now Shiloh takes the bucket of warm bran mash to the field, hooks it on the gate, and then she switches buckets again, full for empty, late in the afternoon.

"Do you want to see how I mix it up?" Mrs. Lima Bean asks, after Shiloh has been feeding Night for a couple of days. "You don't have to. I just thought you might want to do it on your own."

Shiloh shrugs. But she doesn't say no.

"It's like mixing up oatmeal," the woman says.

"I don't like oatmeal. It's gross."

"I never liked oatmeal either." The woman acts like she's telling a secret. "But the horses love this stuff. And know what? We put medicine in it. So he'll get better."

The woman shows her how much medicine to put in,

how to mix it. Shiloh can't believe Mrs. Lima Bean lets her do it on her own. Isn't she worried that Shiloh will get it wrong? That she'll put too much or too little?

One foster freak used to act like she wanted all the kids to bake cookies together, but then she'd get mad if they didn't measure the flour and the sugar exactly right. She'd make them dump it out and start all over again.

"Night is getting used to you," Mrs. Lima Bean says, handing over the bucket of warm mash. "I think he's starting to trust you."

"So?" Shiloh says, but she turns away so Mrs. Lima Bean won't see.

The flicker of a smile.

At the gate she switches buckets. Full for empty. The black horse won't come right away. He keeps his head down. He acts like he doesn't care. But she knows. He wants to gulp it down. He's hungry. Maybe he'll always be hungry. After being starved. Maybe he'll never be able to get enough food.

The black horse snorts hard through his big nose, and then he takes an uneven step forward, another. Limping a little. He stretches his neck out and nudges the bucket, breathes and snorts again. Looks away. Moves closer.

"I don't care if you eat it or not."

The black horse flicks his ears back. He's annoyed. She

can tell. The ears go flat when he's annoyed. The ears always go flat when he's about to scream at Mrs. Lima Bean.

"No skin off my back."

Shiloh turns and starts to walk away. But she hears the bucket clang against the gate. And she can't help it. She turns and wanders back.

Night has his nose in the bucket, chowing down. He lifts his head a moment, flicks his tail, starts eating again.

"I don't know how you stand that stuff," she says. "It's disgusting."

He lifts his head, still chewing mash, grain spilling out between his teeth.

"Don't chew with your mouth open."

Night cocks his ears and then puts his nose back in the bucket.

The sun is bright today. Night's scars are uglier than ever, the ones around his neck thick and raw.

"I have scars. Just like you."

Shiloh glances over toward the barn to make sure Mrs. Lima Bean is still with the other horses. "Wanna see?"

Shiloh puts the bucket down and pulls at the neck of her T-shirt so that her shoulder pokes through.

"It hurt, I guess."

She doesn't touch the scars. She never likes to.

"I don't remember. I was little."

She can't explain. She hasn't. To anyone. How the fear is what she remembers. More than the pain.

And Slade's face. The way he grinned when he was angry so that you wouldn't know at first. That's why you couldn't always get away in time. Because at first you thought he was laughing because he was happy, because he was glad. Because he liked you.

But then you knew.

And maybe there was time to run into the closet. And maybe there wasn't.

But it didn't matter. Because there was never a closet big enough for her mom.

"My mom left him," Shiloh says. "I know she did. She probably had to take out a restraining order on him. That's what people do when somebody's dangerous. She probably had to hide so she could get her head straight."

Night is watching the ground, his ears flicking forward and back. It doesn't matter if he's listening or not. Shiloh tells herself it doesn't matter.

"That's why I can't be with her yet. She has a new apartment and a new baby and she has to hide, but now she wants me to watch my sister so she can get a job. That's all she needs. A good job."

And no Slade.

Shiloh thinks it. Inside her head. She doesn't say his name out loud. Ever. Because if she says his name out loud, it's like he's there with her. It's like he's real and not inside her head, inside her dreams. She knows dreams aren't real. She knows the things inside her head are memories and so they can't hurt her. Not really. But if she says his name out loud, she's not sure what would happen. She's not sure he couldn't find her mom, find her baby sister. She's not sure Slade couldn't find her.

Shiloh looks up at the black horse. He's so big. She doesn't understand how he got his scars. How he would let anyone hurt him like that. With his hooves and his screaming and his legs kicking out. It makes her angry. She can't explain it, but she's angry at the black horse for letting himself get those scars. She turns abruptly away. She walks toward the house. Without looking back.

If she were big, like Night, if she were big and fierce and strong, she would never let anyone near. She would never let anyone touch her ever again.

JESSALYNN

The woman is watching from the back of the barn. A skinny opening where the boards have come loose. She's not spying. She would never spy. But she needs to know. She needs to see for herself.

The girl and the black horse.

Together at the gate.

The girl's mouth is moving. She is talking. More than she has to Jess. More than she has to anyone, probably.

And the black horse is just standing there.

He isn't screaming.

He isn't even looking at Shiloh for the most part. But Jess can tell.

The black horse is listening.

NIGHT

It makes no difference. Who brings the food. The woman or the child. He would still refuse it if he could.

And he could still hurt the child. Even though she has touched him. Even though he has let her touch him.

The child brings the food and she talks to him, and he listens. But he could still hurt her if he wanted to.

Sometimes he wants to. Especially when she leans over the gate to take the empty bucket. Her skinny arm reaching into his field. He could sink his teeth into her flesh, and she would cry, and the bite would leave a mark. And maybe she'd never come to the field again, and that would be okay. He tells himself it would be okay.

Except.

He knows what she sounds like now. Her feet on the gravel. Dragging a little. As if she can't lift her feet all the way.

He knows what she smells like. Fear and anger, and something else mixed in. Something that he doesn't understand, but thinks must be a human child smell.

He knows her voice. Small, like the rest of her, faint, as if she is afraid someone will hear her. But when something startles her, the voice changes. The voice smacks against him. And he wants to stop the voice. But he doesn't.

He could scream at her to make the voice stop.

But he doesn't.

He waits.

And the voice goes soft again.

And every morning, after the sun has come up, he waits. But he tells himself he isn't. Waiting. For her.

Two

SHILOH

"I'm not doing this for you."

There. It's out in the open. Shiloh waits for the woman's face to get angry. But of course it doesn't. The woman only nods.

Shiloh looks away. She just doesn't get it. She can never make the woman mad. And this makes *her* mad, makes her want to kick or punch something.

She could kick the stupid dog that follows the woman everywhere. But the dog always keeps its distance. Like now. It gives her a sideways glance and then speeds up, disappearing into the shadows of the barn.

"It's creepy in here."

Shiloh's voice echoes a little. Something flutters overhead. A bird. A dumb bird is caught in the rafters of the barn. Shiloh watches the bird. She feels trapped too. She wouldn't be in here at all if it weren't for Night.

"I've spent a lot of time in here," the woman's voice comes from around a corner. "I feel at home in a barn."

"That figures," Shiloh mumbles.

"It's always cooler in a barn, in summertime."

Shiloh doesn't answer. The air does feel pretty good in here, but it's creepy just the same.

Two cats slink out from behind a board. One is gray and one is a bunch of different colors. They dart toward Shiloh and swirl like water around her ankles.

Shiloh nudges one with her toe. She's not afraid of cats. They don't have big teeth. You could kick a cat across the room if you needed to, if it tried to scratch.

"There was a woman in our building. She had too many cats. You could smell them all up and down the hallway. We called her the crazy cat lady."

Shiloh stops herself. She doesn't know why she's telling Mrs. Lima Bean anything about her life. Maybe one day she'll be telling somebody that she lived with a crazy horse lady.

"The cats keep the horses company," Mrs. Lima Bean says, her voice a little breathless from tugging a bale of hay from a tall stack. "Horses like to have friends around when they're in the stalls."

"I bet they try to squash the cats flat, just for fun."

The cats have followed close at her heels. Shiloh bends down and pokes at the gray one with her finger. The cat pushes back, trying to get Shiloh to pet him. Now the other one wants to be petted too.

"You'd be surprised," the woman says. "Horses tend to know how strong they are, how big. They're pretty gentle around small creatures. They like cats. I've found the gray one—Jasper—lying right across Mercer Rex's back, taking a snooze."

"I bet Night would squash them flat."

Another cat, all white with blue eyes and a gray tail, darts out from behind the hay. Shiloh stands up. She doesn't have to pet the stupid cats if she doesn't want to.

"What I do is break the bale into two parts," Mrs. Lima Bean is saying. "Like this."

Shiloh watches as the woman takes a knife out from her back pocket and snips the twine that's holding the hay together.

"You carry a knife?" Shiloh asks, and then bites her lip. She doesn't want the woman to think that anything she does is cool or interesting in any way.

"It was my father's," the woman says. She flips the blade back in place and holds it out. "You can look at it, if you like. If you keep it closed."

Shiloh doesn't want to be treated like a baby, told what to do. But she goes forward anyway, and takes the knife and holds it in her hand.

The knife is brown and silver, solid, with a horse engraved on one side and HUTCH engraved on the other. Shiloh thinks about clicking open the blade just to prove to the woman that she can do what she wants.

"Lincoln Andrew Hutchison," the woman says. "That was my father's name. But people called him Hutch."

So?

That's what Shiloh wants to say, but she doesn't. "My dad was in the army," she says instead. "My real dad. Not my mom's boyfriend. My real dad was brave, and he probably had a lot of knives. And guns, too. He left before I was born. He didn't like being pinned down."

"I'm sorry, Shiloh."

"I don't care!" Shiloh doesn't want the woman's pity. "I didn't know him." She could put the knife into her pocket, if she wanted, just to see what the woman would do, but she goes ahead and hands it back.

"I've been giving Night half a bale in the morning, and half in the evening—"

"I'm probably not going to do this every day," Shiloh interrupts.

"That's okay. I know Night appreciates it." The woman grins sideways at her. "He doesn't scream at you so much."

"He doesn't scream at me at all!"

Mrs. Lima Bean keeps grinning, like a dummy.

"There are a couple of wheelbarrows over there," she says, nodding toward the corner. "You can use one to carry the hay out to the field."

Shiloh takes a look. One of the wheelbarrows has brown stuff in it. "Is that what I think it is?" She scrunches up her face. "Gross."

The woman laughs. "I was just about to take that load out to the compost. You can use the other wheelbarrow for the hay."

"That stuff stinks." Putting a hand over her nose.

"I've never minded the smell too much," Mrs. Lima Bean says. "In fact, I think it smells kind of good."

Shiloh stares at her. She *is* crazy.

"That's just plain gross."

"Horses are herbivores."

Shiloh rolls her eyes. She hates when Mrs. Lima Bean acts like she's so smart.

"Herbivores only eat grass and grains. So that's what their manure smells like."

"I don't want to know what their poop smells like!"

Mrs. Lima Bean laughs again, and Shiloh wants to kick her. She could just leave if she wanted to and forget about the stupid hay.

"I'll take this on out," the woman says, heading for the wheelbarrow. "You can get the hay for Night if you want."

Shiloh hesitates. But then she stalks over and grabs hold of the handle. The wheelbarrow is heavier than it looks. It takes a couple of tries before she can roll it straight over to the stacks of hay.

"Don't get used to this," Shiloh calls after the woman. "Just because I'm getting the hay doesn't mean I'm going to start helping you with the gross stuff."

But Mrs. Lima Bean has already disappeared out of the mouth of the barn.

Shiloh clicks her tongue. She'll have to tell her later. She'll have to make sure she understands.

It's a one time thing. Maybe two. At the most. She'll give the black horse some hay today. But who's to say she'll do it again tomorrow? Maybe she'll be gone by then.

Three

JESSALYNN

She knew the rain was coming. She could feel it in her joints, in the small of her back.

The pain doesn't stop her. But it makes everything take longer. The mucking out, the feeding and grooming. The riding is something she has to leave off altogether. At least for a few days. And so the horses stay muddy and restless.

Jess asks the girl if she has a raincoat. The usual shrug for an answer. But Jess goes up into the attic anyway. She finds a dark blue slicker that she must have bought for one of the kids. She can't remember which one, and that bothers her. The arthritis she can bear. The forgetfulness, the dulling of wits, that will be a harder row to hoe.

Jess brings the raincoat downstairs and sponges it off, hangs it by the door. Shiloh ignores it at first. But when Jess comes down from changing out of her wet clothes late in the afternoon, she sees that the raincoat is gone from its peg.

From the kitchen window she watches the dark blue form, hooded against the drizzle, move slowly down the gravel road, scuffing her old white sneakers against the rocks.

The girl needs boots. Jess could take her to Burkman's Feed tomorrow, get her some good sturdy rubber boots. They could stop at Peebles while they're at it and she could get the girl some new clothes. Jess has only seen old T-shirts and jeans, shorts and sneakers. The girl will need warm clothes for fall and winter, she'll need good shoes. She'll be starting school soon.

Not here, of course.

The residential treatment center is closer to Lexington. She'll be there in less than a week.

Ms. Brown, the social worker, called last evening. While the girl was still outside with Night.

Shiloh's place at the RTC has opened. Ms. Brown wanted to know if she should come out to tell Shiloh herself. Jess said no, she would do it.

But she hasn't yet. And she's not sure why.

She watches the blue raincoat reach the gate, watches the black horse move forward.

Maybe Shiloh could come on the weekends, to visit Night.

Maybe . . .

Something tugs, something vague, but persistent.
Maybe . . .

She lets the *something* trail away. She's never asked for a permanent placement. In all the time she's been doing foster care. She's always thought of herself as a port in the storm. Safe and secure, but temporary.

SHILOH

The woman is always singing or humming. The same tune. Familiar, although Shiloh is sure she's never heard the song before she came here.

An old-timey kind of song. Something a grandma might sing. Not a mom, *her* mom.

Shiloh's mom sang songs off the radio. Rock and roll. Never country. She hated country music. She said country music was all sad-sack songs. People wailing on and on about broken hearts and being lonesome. She didn't want to hear sad-sack songs. She wanted to listen to something that raised you up, made you feel alive.

She'd keep Shiloh home from school. On the bad days. When sunglasses weren't enough to hide the bruises on her mom's face. When her mom was too sore.

They'd lie in bed and listen to the radio because the TV

was busted. And her mom would turn the music up and sing at the top of her lungs, and the old lady next door would bang on the wall with her broom, but her mom just kept singing.

Those were the best days.

Because Shiloh didn't have to go to dumb old school.

Because Shiloh had her mom to herself. All alone in the bed. And she would sing along with her mom, but she knew she didn't have her mom's voice. Her mom could hit all the high notes. She could sound exactly like anybody singing on the radio. Her mom could have been a rock star, and then they would have been rich and her mom would never have needed somebody like Slade because she'd have had all the money in the world. And they would be together. Just the two of them. The three of them now. Because of the baby. And that would be okay.

Shiloh gets up from the bed and goes to the window. It's after *together time*. She can hear the woman's voice, singing, as she moves around the kitchen downstairs. The voice is muffled, of course, but Shiloh knows. It's the same tune the woman always sings. Spooky-sounding. Slow.

Shiloh reaches out and puts a hand to the window. The rain is running down the glass in squiggly little lines.

She was going to run away last night. But the rain didn't stop. She doesn't want to be a baby, but she doesn't want to get wet and stay wet. She might get sick, and then what good would she be? To her mom? To her sister?

She wonders about Night. Out in the rain. She can't see him because it's dark, but she knows he's there. Wet and muddy. Standing in his corner. Staring at the fence.

During the day he rolls around in the muddy field. And when he gets up, he really looks like a monster. All black and slimy.

But funny, too.

The black horse rolls all the way over in the mud, feet straight up in the air, and she laughs. She can't help it. She wonders what it would feel like to roll around and get that muddy with nobody to care.

One time she was playing in a mud puddle out in the yard, and Slade came home and he yanked her up by one arm and carried her screaming into the apartment. He shoved her into the bathtub and turned the shower on full blast.

The water kept getting hotter, and her arm ached where he'd yanked it, and she doesn't remember anything else.

But she never played in mud puddles again. Ever.

Down below, the woman's voice stops, and then starts up again. Still muffled.

The sound is clearer when Shiloh opens her bedroom door a crack. The words to the song are hard to follow.

But Shiloh listens anyway. She slides down on the floor, her back leaning into the door frame, and tries to figure it out. What the song is about.

night

His strength is coming back. He feels it. A little more each day.

Now when the mare runs along her fence, Night runs too. Just to show her. She's not so fast.

It still hurts of course. But the pain is not fire like it used to be. Fire everywhere.

And his skin. The itching and the burning is not so bad. Especially with the rain beating down on him.

During the day he rolls around on the ground, scratching his back, covering himself in mud.

And the child laughs.

At first he didn't know. He didn't remember. About laughter. He didn't think he would care.

But now, during the day, he rolls in the mud, legs to the sky. And the laughter escapes out of her, and he stops, and then he rolls again, waiting for the sound.

Laughter. Hers.

Four

JESSALYNN

The girl begins to eat without the usual remarks about her lousy cooking. Silence for most of the meal. But it's a different silence from before. Not so tense, not so charged, like the air right before a summer thunderstorm.

Jess hasn't had to go to Shiloh's room in the middle of the night nearly as much. There's been less screaming, less whimpering in her sleep.

Is it because of the black horse?

Jess wonders. She hopes.

Connection.

The beginning.

But only the beginning. Probably it's too little too late.

Jess still hasn't told Shiloh that she's leaving in a week's time. She should do it tonight. Now.

"Night should go in the barn like the other horses do." Shiloh breaks the silence. "He's wet all the time."

Jess glances toward the window. She's thankful for the rain even with the pain in her joints. This time last year the place was a desert.

"Horses don't mind the rain," Jess says.

"But you put Seph up at night. You put the others up."

"That's true." Jess nods. "But Night was kept cooped up inside a barn so long, he's probably happier out in the open." She pauses, clears her throat. "When it starts getting cold, he'll need to go into the barn. Hopefully he'll be ready for somebody to lead him by then."

"He wouldn't let *you* lead him there, that's for sure," Shiloh says. "Not in a million years."

"Well, maybe he'd let *you*. Maybe—"

Jess catches herself. She doesn't know why she said that. The girl will be gone by the time it gets cold.

"I won't be here that long," Shiloh says sharply, as if reading Jess's thoughts. "I told you before. My mom's waiting for me. She needs me. I have a baby sister." Her voice is quieter now. "That's better than any old horse."

Jess takes a breath. This is the moment. To tell Shiloh that she's leaving sooner than she thinks.

"I'm done," Shiloh announces. She picks up her plate and glass, and takes them to the sink. Such a big change from the first couple of weeks.

"Thanks," Jess says, but that's all she manages before the girl leaves the room.

After she's taken her own dishes to the sink, Jess wipes down the table and the counters, gives Bella some scraps in her bowl. She assumes the girl has gone on up to her room, so it's a surprise when she finds her in the living room, standing at the fireplace.

"Who's this?"

The girl is looking at the photographs on the mantel.

"Me," Jess answers, moving closer, sure that Shiloh will simply shrug and walk away. "At a hunter show."

"What's a hunter show?"

"A riding competition."

"You were young!" Shiloh says. As if such a thing isn't possible. "That must have been a million years ago."

Jess nods. "It sure feels that way."

"You weren't so bad-looking then."

"Thanks," Jess says, surprised. "But the real looker is Lorelei."

The girl squints at the picture.

"The horse."

Shiloh clicks her tongue, rolls her eyes, but she stays where she is, as if she wants to know more.

"She was quite a gal," Jess says. "We loved showing what we could do together."

"That's a big trophy," Shiloh remarks sharply, a challenge.

"We collected a lot of trophies that year."

"Where are they, then?" Shiloh obviously doesn't believe her.

Jess thinks for a moment. It's been years since she's been reminded of the trophies. Years since they've seen the light of day.

"In the barn, I suppose. I have a lot of boxes in there, old things."

"My mom got a trophy once," Shiloh says. "For being beautiful. The most beautiful one at the fair. She could have been Miss America if she wanted to be." She moves on to the next photograph. "Who's the guy?"

"That's Rob. My husband."

Shiloh turns to stare at her. She obviously doesn't believe Jess was ever married. "No way."

"Way," Jess replies, a response the last foster kid taught her.

Shiloh scowls at that, but turns back to the picture. "He's not around anymore." A statement, not a question. "Did he just take off one day?"

"He died," Jess says simply. She can say it simply now. There was a time she could not. "He and my daughter, Maggie. They were in a car accident. When Maggie was here visiting us. After she was all grown up. They were just going to the store. Just a quick trip. And there was a man driving a truck. He had been drinking." Jess pauses. "Rob died right away. Maggie lived a little longer, about a week in the hospital. She was going to have a baby. But the baby was too little yet to survive. Maggie was too badly hurt. They both died."

Jess doesn't expect the girl to have anything to say to that. Maybe she shouldn't have told her. It's a lot to handle all at once. A tragedy. Although Jess has never allowed herself to consider her life tragic for very long. Terrible things happen. Good things too. That's the way life is.

"Where's Maggie's picture?" Shiloh demands, as if she still doesn't quite believe Jess.

"I keep one by my bed upstairs."

Jess takes the old bandanna out of her back pocket, where she usually keeps it. The photographs are dusty, the old mantel clock, too, and so she gives everything a quick swipe. She doesn't dust as much as she should. Not like her granny. Her granny lived until she was ninety-five and dusted up to her dying day.

"Sorry."

Jess nearly misses it, the word comes out so quick and soft.

"Thank you," Jess manages before the girl turns and disappears upstairs.

. . .

NIGHT

Rain was only something he heard. Before. Inside the walls of the barn. A few drops now and then. From the leaky roof.

But not like this.

Rain. Day after day.

Hard against his back. Taking away the stink and the heat and the fire. Taking away the pain.

Washing him clean.

Rain.

He wonders. What it is about the rain that makes him feel new again, alive? After all, the rain is only water.

Part three: Chains

One

JESSALYNN

Brrrr-

The familiar sound. Annoying, like a lone mosquito.

-nnnnnnng.

Jerking her out of sleep.

Brrrr-

If she ignored the sound, would it stop? How many rings would it take to stop? She doesn't have an answering machine.

-nnnnnnng!

Old-fashioned and impractical, she knows. Stubborn, Nita calls it. But here's how Jess sees it: If somebody wants to get hold of her, they'll call back when she's home.

Brrrr-

"Hello?"

In the end it's too hard to ignore a ringing phone, in case it *is* an emergency of some kind.

"Hello?"

The usual emptiness. On the other end. Some breathing starting up. Raspy-sounding. A clinking. Ice cubes, maybe?

"You really must have the wrong number."

The clock says it's three. In the morning. Not exactly the same time as the other nights, but pretty close.

"Or else you're doing this to be funny. It's not funny. It's becoming a nuisance now. Please stop." She pauses, and then says it again, more firmly. "Please, stop."

After she's hung up, she sinks her head back onto the pillow, stares up into the dark. Bella's warm body shifts along one leg. Jess thinks she'll get up like usual, go check on the girl, see to Night. But her body feels too heavy tonight, too hard to move. She closes her eyes, and slips soundlessly back into sleep.

SHILOH

Brrrrnnnnnnng!

Eyes popping open.

Brrrrnnnnnnng!

A phone ringing. Not just inside her dream anymore. A real phone.

Brrrrnnnnnnng!

The girl jerks up and out of bed. Her heart is thudding so loud she can't hear anything else.

Brrrrnnnnnnng!

Except the phone.

It's her mom calling. She knows. Even though it's nowhere near her birthday. Who else would call in the middle of the night?

Brrrr-

The sound is cut off, and the girl wants to scream. But she makes herself keep quiet as she opens the door and tiptoes down the hall.

She knows there's a phone downstairs, in the kitchen. But there's another phone in the woman's bedroom.

And so she waits. And she hears it. A voice. Mrs. Lima Bean's voice.

Shiloh holds her breath and listens.

The woman is telling the person on the other end to stop calling in the middle of the night, that it's a nuisance. To please stop.

Shiloh wants to crash through the door and yank the phone away from the woman.

But she doesn't, can't. Because the woman hangs up before she even has a chance. The call is over.

Shiloh waits to see what the woman will do. She knows the woman doesn't always sleep through the night. She's heard her get up and go down the stairs, move around the kitchen.

But tonight the woman stays in bed. After a few minutes Shiloh hears a light snoring.

Will her mom try to call again? Tonight? Tomorrow? When?

And why is her mom calling when it's not her birthday?

Maybe it's not her mom at all. Maybe it's a total stranger.

But it *must* be her mom. It *has* to be.

And she's calling to say that she's ready. She's ready for Shiloh to come to her.

Shiloh knows it's a secret. Her mom calling. She knows her mom isn't supposed to call at all. Ever. Her mom's not even supposed to know where Shiloh is.

And yet.

She *has* called. She *has* known. Every time Shiloh's moved. Every time she's in a new place, on her birthday. Her mom has called. Somehow she's found out.

And now, Shiloh's been sleeping through the calls. Like a dumb baby. Shiloh messed up. But her mom has to give her another chance, right? She *has* to.

Shiloh goes back down the hall to her room. She ducks into the closet to check the suitcase, to make sure everything is packed, ready to go.

The phone will ring tomorrow. Shiloh knows it will. And she'll be there to answer it.

Two

JESSALYNN

The sun is shining bright and cheerful through the window when the woman opens her eyes. She can feel it instantly. The stiffness is gone. The rain has cleared.

"Lazybones," she mutters to herself when she sees the clock. "Why didn't you wake me up, huh?" She gives Bella a gentle nudge.

Downstairs, Jess rinses out the coffeepot. No dirty cereal bowl in the sink. No sign of Shiloh out the window.

Jess listens for sounds overhead. Nothing. And so while the coffee is perking, she heads back up the stairs. She stands at the closed door to Shiloh's bedroom, taps softly, and then harder.

No response, and so she eases the door open just a crack.

The girl is lying with the quilt pulled all the way up despite the sunny warmth of the room. Only the pale strands of her hair are showing.

"Shiloh?"

The girl doesn't move, doesn't respond.

Did she have a nightmare? One that Jess didn't hear? Was she frightened and awake in the middle of the night?

Jess takes a step into the room. The girl shifts under the quilt, but doesn't wake.

Strange how they both slept late today. But then again, maybe they both needed it. So many restless nights.

Jess turns and pulls the door closed behind her. Back downstairs she drinks her cup of black coffee and heads out toward the barn. She can hear the horses calling to her, asking what's taken her so long.

SHILOH

She listens to the woman's footsteps, later than usual, heading down to the kitchen. And then coming back up again. She pulls the covers over her head when she hears the knock, the woman calling her name. She acts like she's sleeping when the woman opens the door.

After the woman is gone, Shiloh sits up. And then she's watching the same old thing. The woman walking outside with the dog, disappearing into the barn.

She was starting to like it. The same thing every morning. A routine.

But now just watching the woman and the dog makes her mad.

How can somebody do the same thing day after day? Over and over again?

It's good she's leaving. She won't miss anything about this place.

Except.

She looks past the barn, toward the far field. The black horse is just now leaving his corner, walking to the gate, slow and careful like the woman.

When he gets to the gate, he lifts his head and sniffs at the air. He turns toward the house, ears all the way up, listening.

Is he waiting for her?

No, that's stupid. He's just a horse. He's hungry, that's all. He wants his bucket of food. It doesn't matter who brings it to him.

"Not today, buddy." Shiloh makes her voice hard. "Not from me."

She turns away from the window. She ignores the feeling in her chest. She doesn't even know what it means.

•   •   •

NIGHT

The sun rises, and the child is not there, and it doesn't matter.

He tells himself.

It does not. Matter.

When the woman finally walks over with the bucket of warm mash, he rushes at her. He won't let her hook the feed over the gate. He kicks at the metal. He screams. He snaps his teeth at her.

And then he goes back to his corner.

He will not turn. Even if he hears the child's footsteps on the gravel.

He will not turn. And he will not let her touch him again.

Three

JESSALYNN

"Shiloh?"

Jess waits, listening at the closed door. "Shiloh, are you in there?"

"Where else would I be?"

Jess feels relief despite the sharpness. "Are you okay?"

No answer.

"Are you feeling okay?"

"No. My stomach hurts."

"Oh, dear. I'll get you some ginger ale."

"Just leave me alone."

Jess hesitates, unsure whether to go ahead and barge in.

"There's a wastebasket in there, if you need to upchuck."

Silence.

"Do you feel like you need to upchuck?"

"I don't even know what that means!" the girl shouts.

"Throw up. Do you feel like you might throw up?"

"Yeah, I guess." A pause. Not shouting anymore. "Just leave me alone. I want to sleep."

Jess goes ahead with her chores, but she doesn't venture too far from the house. In the middle of the afternoon she taps on the door again, and the girl says she can come in.

"I brought you some crackers and some ginger ale. That always makes me feel better when I have an upset stomach."

The girl doesn't respond. She is lying flat on the bed, staring up at the ceiling. Her face is paler than usual. Her hair is damp with sweat.

"It's pretty hot in here," Jess says.

The girl shrugs, turns her head away.

"I'd like to see if you have a fever, okay?"

No response. Jess wants to be careful. The only time she's actually ever touched the girl is in her sleep.

"I'm going to put my hand on your forehead, all right?"

Shiloh shrugs again, and Jess reaches out, lays her palm just below the hairline.

"A little warm," Jess says. Her hand brushes at some strands of hair, she can't help it.

"I might throw up on you," Shiloh warns.

"I can handle it. I've dealt with worse."

"Yeah, you play with horse poop all the time."

Jess chuckles. She goes to turn on the fan near the

window, positions it so it'll stir the air without blowing directly onto the bed.

"I'm sorry I don't have air-conditioning."

"Yeah, this place is a dump."

"Actually, I never liked air-conditioning. Don't like all that frosty air."

Jess glances out the window. Instead of leaving right away she sits down on the chair near the bed. Something is tugging at her and she can't quite put her finger on it.

"Is anything wrong, Shiloh?"

She waits.

"Anything you want to tell me about?"

"My stomach hurts. I told you that already. Are you getting senile?"

"Sometimes I think I am," Jess answers with a sigh. "And I hate that. I hate the idea of forgetting things."

"Why?"

The girl turns to look at Jess. Really look at her. There's the usual sullenness, the scowl. But there's something else, too. Jess is sure of it. A glimmer of something behind the toughness.

"I'd want to forget things. If I was you," the girl says, "I'd want to forget about your family dying like they did."

Jess is surprised. It takes her a minute to think of what to say.

"If I forgot about them dying, I'd forget the rest of it too. The good times. The wonderful times."

The girl turns her face back to the wall. She crosses her arms over her chest.

"What if there's nothing good to remember?"

It's a fair question. If Jess had a past like Shiloh's, she'd probably want to forget too.

"Is there something upsetting you?" Jess tries again. She can't shake the nagging feeling that it's more than a stomach-ache.

The girl doesn't answer right away. And when she does, her voice doesn't have the usual edge to it.

"I just want to be alone. I told you already. I feel sick and I just want to be alone."

"Okay, then."

Jess gives up. For the moment. She rises to her feet and heads for the door.

"You know, Shiloh," she says, turning, "Night's been watching for you. He didn't like it at all when I brought him his food. I think he's missed you today."

The girl keeps her face to the wall.

"I'm not your slave," she mumbles. "I don't have to feed him if I don't want to. It's not my job."

A sinking. Inside her chest.

"No, Shiloh, it's not your job."

Jess turns and leaves the room, closing the door softly behind her.

SHILOH

All day she waits. But the phone does not ring. And it does not ring.

And the woman hovers nearby like she's really some old grandma. Bringing in more ginger ale, and crackers and a bowl of soup.

Shiloh eats it all, because she's starving, but she keeps telling the woman that she thinks she's going to throw up.

"I'll have to call the doctor tomorrow," the woman says, checking her forehead again. "If your stomach isn't any better."

So Shiloh has to be careful. She needs to be sick but not too sick. Not sick enough for the woman to have to take her somewhere.

Because then she'd miss the call for sure.

When Mrs. Lima Bean finally goes out to the barn, Shiloh heads down the hallway. Into the woman's room.

There are more photographs here, hanging on the walls. Mostly horses. Some old people too. Dressed in old-fashioned clothes.

Shiloh perches on the edge of the bed. She picks up the phone and listens to the dial tone to be sure, hangs up.

There's a small framed photo on the table, beside the phone. A little girl with blond hair, standing in a field, holding something blurry in her hands.

Maggie. That's who it is. Shiloh knows right away. She picks up the picture.

The little girl has a bow in her hair. And it's flowers she's holding. They're blurry because she's trying to give flowers to the person behind the camera. And she's laughing. Shiloh can tell. Maggie is laughing.

Brrrrnnnnnng!

The sound makes her jump, makes her drop the photograph to the floor.

Brrrrnnnnnng!

Shiloh can't believe it. She stares at the phone, wide-eyed.

Brrrrnnnnnng!

Then she grabs at the receiver, fumbling with the talk button. She stops herself just in time. Before she cries out like a baby. She stops herself, and waits.

"Hello? Hello? Mrs. DiLima, is that you?"

A voice. On the other end. Not her mom's. But a voice she knows anyway.

"Hello? This is Ms. Brown calling. Hello? Is that you, Mrs. DiLima?"

Shiloh wants to slam the phone down hard, against the table. She wants to scream at the state lady to hang up.

"Hello? Mrs. DiLima?"

"It's Shiloh."

The words slide out. She doesn't know why. She should just hang up.

"Oh!"

A pause, and then the cheerful laughter Shiloh hates.

"Hi there, Shiloh. I was just a little surprised that you answered the phone! But I'm glad you did! How are you?"

Shiloh doesn't let any words escape this time.

"I hear things have gone really well there."

A flash of anger. Fast and hot. Like a match bursting to flame.

The woman has been spying on her. Reporting back to the state lady. Spying and telling secrets. Lies, probably. Like every other foster freak.

"I think that's terrific! I'm so glad it all worked out. I said you'd like the horses!"

Shiloh hates the voice. So bright and cheerful. She wants to hang up. She wants to kick something.

And that's when she sees it. Maggie's little-girl face lying on the floor, a crack running straight down the middle of her smile.

"Is Mrs. DiLima nearby? I was hoping to speak with her."

"She's outside."

"Okay, then." A pause. "Well, just tell her I called, okay? I wanted to remind her that I'll be there Friday, around noon, to pick you up. We'll get you all settled in at the center. You'll be starting back to school next week. Won't that be exciting? A new school."

"What?" Shiloh blurts out. The state lady must be confused.

"I know, time has really flown, hasn't it? I can't believe it either. But school will be starting up next week, and we need to get you settled in at the center before that. You'll be rooming with a girl just your age. You'll be in the same class. Isn't that great? It's all worked out so well. . . ."

The state lady keeps talking, but Shiloh doesn't hear anything else.

A punch in the stomach, that's what it's like. She's been punched in the stomach before, by other foster kids. But she's usually been able to punch back.

Not this time. All she can do is sit, and take it.

She can't believe the woman didn't tell her that the state lady was coming on Friday. She can't believe the woman acted like she wanted Shiloh to stay and help with the black horse when she knew that would never happen.

And she can't believe she's crying. Now. This very minute. Like a baby. A big fat crybaby.

It's not like she ever thought she'd be staying here, with the woman. It's not like she ever wanted to.

Shiloh looks down at Maggie's face, the crack running through her smile.

"So, I'll see you Friday. Around noon, okay, Shiloh?"

Shiloh doesn't answer. She hangs up before the state lady can say good-bye.

There's a loud *snap* as she stands up. She can feel the rest of the glass shattering, the frame breaking under her shoe.

She leaves the mess where it is and goes back to her room. She still wants to break something. So she takes the woman's precious book out from under her bed. She rips through the rest of the pages. Fistfuls at a time. The thin pieces of paper flutter to the floor, broken wings. Shiloh doesn't bother to stop and pick them up, to hide what she's done. She rips and rips until there's nothing left to destroy.

Four

JESSALYNN

Jessalynn has made a decision. She will call the social worker. This very afternoon. And ask for more time. She should have done it sooner. She hopes it's not too late.

Coming in from the chores, she heads up the stairs to make the call. Bella lopes ahead, through the open door, and so it's the dog who finds it first, sniffing and poking her long nose tentatively at the clinky shards of glass.

"No!" Jess warns sharply, and immediately Bella lifts her head, backs away.

At first Jess thinks it's simply an accident. A breeze through the open window. Knocking the photograph of Maggie to the floor.

But the window isn't open. And nothing else on the bedside table is disturbed.

Why?

Jess eases down onto her knees. The sharp edges of glass

have slit the photo nearly in two. The photo Jess loves most of all, the one that doesn't have a copy, the negative lost long ago.

Why?

Jess eases the photo out from the broken frame. She takes it with her as she heads back out the door, down the hall.

She has to know.

Why.

SHILOH

Footsteps. The door to the bedroom flung open without a knock.

"Shiloh!"

The woman's voice, sharper than she's ever heard it. A gasp as she takes it all in. The destruction. The torn pages of her precious book. Scattered across the floor.

Shiloh's teeth begin to chatter. She wedges herself tighter into the corner.

"Shiloh!"

A pause.

"Shiloh!"

The door to the closet swings open, and the woman is standing there, mouth set in a hard line, face flushed.

Shiloh grins, despite the chattering of her teeth. This is what she's wanted. All along. For the woman to shout back, to lash out. It makes her relieved somehow, and at the same time it makes her afraid.

"It's a stupid book," Shiloh hears herself say. "A baby book." She crosses her arms over her knees, hugs them tighter. She will not come out on her own. The woman will have to drag her out.

"But . . . why? Why did you tear it all up? Why didn't you just give it back to me if you didn't like it?"

The woman's voice isn't slow and steady like usual. The words are rushed, rising. One eye is twitching off to the side; the other is a laser beam.

Shiloh juts out her chin. She can't think of what to say. With the one eye burning a hole into her. She can't think of a reason.

And then she does.

"Because I hate you!"

Finding the words, plucking them from out of nowhere. Repeating them.

"I hate you!"

Like a fist punching. Right in the gut.

"I'm glad the state lady is coming! I'm glad she's coming to get me! I hate you, and I never want to see you and your stupid horses again!"

The woman opens her mouth, closes it. Like a fish. A dumb fish out of water. Open. Close. Open.

Shiloh laughs, more like a hiccup, teeth still chattering. Her eyes flash down to what the woman is holding.

"I'm glad I'm not your daughter."

Shiloh takes a breath. Part of her wants to stop. From saying the rest. But she can't.

"Maggie's probably better off dead. With you for a mom. Somebody who cares more about horses than people."

Shiloh waits. She braces herself. For a slap across the face, a punch, a kick even. That's what the woman *should* do. Shiloh isn't sorry for what she's done, what she's said, she knows she's not, but the woman should *make* her sorry.

Instead the woman turns. Away from the closet, away from Shiloh. She turns and walks to the middle of the room, hands on hips. She stands there, gazing down at the torn pages on the floor, shaking her head back and forth, slow and careful, as if somebody has asked her a question and her answer is no.

Shiloh waits and waits. For screaming and yelling. For the woman to tell her that she hates her back.

But the woman doesn't say a word.

And then she's gone. Just like that.

Shiloh keeps on waiting. Hunched in her corner of the closet. Because maybe the woman will come back. With a switch or something. That's what one of the other foster freaks used to use to punish her. A switch from a weeping willow tree.

But the woman doesn't come back and doesn't come back, and Shiloh bangs her fist against the wall where all the bad words are written. She keeps on banging until her hand hurts enough to make her stop.

Crybaby.

Hands up to her face now, cheeks wet as rain.

What a dumb crybaby she is!

And worst of all: She doesn't even understand, she doesn't even know what the woman has done to make her cry.

JESSALYNN

Jess doesn't bother with the shards of glass. Just like she didn't bother with the pages of the ruined book. She is too tired, suddenly. She is weary to her very bones.

And so she lies down on the bed—something she rarely does during the day. She sets Maggie's photograph face-down on the pillow beside her and closes her eyes.

She has never given up. Ever. She has always seen a thing through. But this time, maybe she *is* too old. Maybe what she has to offer—an extra room, a chance to be around horses, a safe place—maybe it's just not enough. Maybe it would never be enough. For a girl as angry, as hurt as Shiloh. And maybe this is what getting old means. Knowing when it's time to give up.

SHILOH

The last wooden step groans beneath her sneaker, and Shiloh freezes. She waits, breath caught inside her chest, listening, listening with all her might.

Silence. Nothing more. And darkness, behind her, up the stairs.

And so she keeps moving. Through the living room. Into the kitchen to grab some food. She'll be gone by the time the woman wakes up in the morning. She'll never see this place again.

It doesn't matter. What the woman said. Later. After leaving Shiloh alone for so long.

"I'm sorry."

Bringing Shiloh her supper on a tray. Leaving it on the table by the bed.

"I should have told you about Ms. Brown coming. I'm sorry."

As if that made a difference. The stupid word "sorry." The tray of food.

"We'll talk about everything in the morning. Okay? We'll talk about it tomorrow."

As if Shiloh would hang around. Just to talk. As if she cared what the woman had to say.

She doesn't care.

And so she doesn't even know why she bothered. Picking up the pages of the woman's stupid book, smoothing out the wrinkles, sticking them back inside the ruined cover.

She doesn't know why she left the whole thing, like a present, on the bed, for the woman to find in the morning.

Inside the dark kitchen Shiloh sets the suitcase down. She opens the refrigerator and pulls out some cheese and ham and hamburger buns. She puts it all into a plastic grocery bag and stuffs it into her suitcase.

She's just reaching for a box of cereal in one of the cabinets when the wall phone next to her starts to ring.

Brrrrnnnnnnng!

Instantly she grabs at the phone. Before it can ring again, before it can wake the woman.

"Mom?"

She says it even though she knows she's not supposed to.

"Mom?"

She waits, waits for the click. Her mom showing her that she's made a mistake. But all she hears is breathing. Heavy, raspy-sounding. Like her mom has a cold.

"Mom? Are you okay?"

Nothing. Just the breathing. Shiloh bites her lip until it bleeds. She doesn't know what she'll do if her mom hangs up now.

"I'll help you if you're sick. I'll help with the baby. And then you can get better. And you can get a job. And we'll all be together."

She waits. She can wait forever if she has to. But she hopes she doesn't have to.

"Mom?"

There's only a soft grunt. But at least it's something.

Maybe her mom is so sick she's lost her voice.

"If I tell you where I am, will you come to get me? Tonight? I've got to leave. Tonight. The state lady is coming day after tomorrow."

Another grunt, louder this time, so that Shiloh's heart stops. And the sweat breaks out on her skin. She's shivering even though it's a warm night.

Is it Slade? Is he playing a trick on her?

Shiloh nearly hangs up herself, she's suddenly so frightened. But she stops.

No. It's not Slade. Her mom wouldn't be with Slade

anymore. Couldn't. Shiloh has to believe that. Even though her mom's never said. But of course her mom's never said anything. Before last time. Before the baby cried, and she told Shiloh. How she has a sister.

"You could come to get me. It's not too far."

Shiloh has to believe. That it's her mom on the other end.

"The address is 1236 Culver Pike. It took, like, an hour to get here from downtown."

Shiloh hears another cough, heavy and wet. Her mom must be really sick. Maybe she's too sick to make it.

"Will you come tonight? I'm ready. I have to go."

A sound. In between a cough and a grunt.

Yes.

That's what Shiloh hears anyway.

Yes.

"1236 Culver Pike." Repeating it to be sure. "There's a sign out front. DiLima Stables. Because the woman keeps horses. She has this one horse. He's crazy and mean. He's the biggest horse ever. They call him Night because he's all black—"

Click.

The line goes dead. Shiloh stares at the phone in her hand. She stares until the dial tone starts bleating at her. And then she hangs up.

Her mom had to rush. That's all. So that she can make

it tonight. She had to hang up. But she's coming. Shiloh knows.

Her mom is coming for her. Tonight.

How long will it take?

An hour at least. Maybe longer. Because of the distance. Because of the dark.

Shiloh didn't notice before, but now she sees. It's extra dark outside. No stars. No moon. Just dark. Pitch black.

Shiloh lets herself out through the kitchen door. She sets the suitcase on the porch and sits down to wait. Maybe she should go to the road, but it's so dark outside. She'll wait until she sees headlights. She'll wait until she's sure.

But she *is* sure.

Her mom will come with her baby sister. And they'll all be together, and nobody will ever split them apart again.

JESSALYNN

Jess hears the phone ring once, then stop.

She waits, but there is only silence. As she slips back into sleep, she hopes the baby is still there, waiting for her inside the dream.

• • •

NIGHT

Tight inside the rush of bodies, he can smell rage and joy. He can smell fear. He does not know which makes his legs go faster. All he knows is that he has to fight.

And so he fights.

And around the turn the man lets him go. A little. Bodies still in the way, but he can see the open spaces.

Open.

Close.

Open.

Close.

It's that quick. Too quick to think about. Time only to move.

And that's what he does.

Move.

One by one the bodies fall away. Until only two remain.

And still he fights and fights and fights, and the man lets him go at last. And there are two bodies.

One.

Open space.

He listens for the sound. The roaring of the crowd. Terrible and beautiful. The sound of winning.

But he doesn't hear it and he doesn't hear it. And then he hears something else.

Clank-clank.

And in the darkness, he does not know. Is he back? Inside the past? Is this only a dream?

More like a nightmare.

A nightmare he thought he'd left behind.

SHILOH

Her eyes pop open in the dark. She can't believe she fell asleep. Head against the wood of the porch. Something startling her awake.

A sound.

A light.

How long has she been asleep?

A light!

She pushes herself up, rubs at her eyes, strains to see in the dark.

A light. Moving through the trees. At the far end of the driveway. Small and quick. A flashlight.

Shiloh picks up the suitcase and steps off the porch. She knows the driveway, even in the pitch black. Knows how many steps it takes to get to the road. She walks along the edge of the gravel, in the grass, so the rocks won't crunch beneath her feet.

Mom!

She wants to scream at the top of her lungs. But that would ruin everything.

Mom!

The flashlight is moving. Just up ahead. Shiloh keeps walking, waiting for the light to swerve this way, for the light to find her.

Clank-clank.

She stops. Dead in her tracks.

Clank-clank.

A sound she doesn't understand.

Clank-clank.

Like chains rattling together.

"Mom?"

Just a whisper.

"Mom?"

The flashlight hasn't stopped moving, but it's curving away from her now. It's heading for the far field. So Shiloh speeds up.

"Mom?"

A little louder this time.

"Mom?"

The light jerks her way, slashing at the dark. Then disappearing. Snuffed out.

Shiloh waits. She hears the clanking again, and the

skin prickles up along the back of her neck.

"Mom?"

She knows her voice is small and scared, like a baby, but she can't help it. She's not sure anymore. She's not sure it's her mom who's out there.

The light flashes on suddenly, closer now, sweeping across the grass, finding her.

"Mom?"

The light is blinding. She puts her arm up to shield her eyes. She hears the rustle of grass, the person with the light coming closer.

And that's when it hits her. The smell. Sweet and sharp. Bitter.

She takes a step back, but the ground is unsteady. The suitcase drops from her hand. She leaves it where it is.

The smell is whiskey.

The smell is Slade.

She turns to run. But she's not fast enough.

Big rough hands, grabbing her by the shoulders, yanking. An arm hooked around her neck, jerking tighter.

She is being dragged backward, along the ground, heels digging into mud. She can smell whiskey and sweat mixed together. She can smell something else, too, something she doesn't know. Sharp, metallic.

Clank-clank.

She feels something cold slink against her leg.

Clank-clank.

And then she hears a sound she recognizes. The creak of a gate, swinging open.

The arm hooked around her neck loosens a little. So she tries to fight, tries to push away, but that only makes the grip tighten again, and she is gasping for air, she cannot breathe.

And so she cannot scream. But who would hear her, anyway? In the middle of nowhere?

Jess. That's who. Jess would hear the scream and she'd come running. Because even though Jess is old, she's tough. And Shiloh knows—all at once she knows—Jess is the only one who can help her.

Clank-clank.

But that doesn't matter now. She cannot scream. She cannot breathe. She is gasping for air, falling into darkness.

Falling. Sinking.

She cannot. Breathe.

Rrrhhhraaaa!

A scream, piercing the darkness.

Rrrhhhraaaa!

And the earth, rumbling beneath her feet, tipping.

Rrrhhhraaaa!

Without warning she snaps forward. Hands and knees hitting ground. The air rushes back into her lungs. Too sudden and sharp. She is gasping, coughing.

But she is breathing.

Rrrrhhhraaaa!

She needs to get up, run, but the ground is unsteady and something big and fast rushes by in the dark.

Clank-clank!

And the sound, like a chain.

Clank-clank!

Shiloh knows she has to run. She needs to get away. But her legs are rubbery; they will not hold. She stumbles forward again, head striking the ground, splinters of light, like fireworks behind her lids, pain.

"I'll show you who's boss!"

A voice. Booming out from somewhere behind her. A voice she does not know.

"I'll show you!"

She glances back into the darkness.

"I'm the boss, yessirree."

And a face appears out of nowhere, caught inside the jittery beam of the flashlight, gone just as quick.

Not Slade.

"This is it, boy. Just you and me."

The man is not Slade.

"Thought they could steal you from me, didn't they? Well, I'll show 'em. I'll show you, too."

Clank-clank.

Something glints in the jerking light.

Clank-clank.

And Shiloh starts to crawl. Away from the man who is not Slade. Head throbbing now, with every move; throat raw and burning. She cannot stand, cannot run, but she can crawl.

Clank-clank.

Chains. The sound *is* chains. And she doesn't understand, but she keeps crawling anyway. And she feels a rush of air. Brushing along her back. The beating of wings.

Rrrrhhhraaaa!

The scream and the same rumbling as before. Dark and heavy. Thunder rolling. Up from the ground.

Rrrrhhhraaaa!

The scream, and then another voice.

"Aaaaaaaaaaahhh!"

The man's voice. The man who is not Slade.

"Aaaaaaaaaaahhh!"

Different now. Frightened. Small.

Rrrrhhhraaaa!

A crack, like lightning. Sudden and sharp and final. A bolt of lightning splitting a tree in two.

And then silence.

Shiloh braces herself for more, but there is nothing. Only darkness. And quiet.

She tries pushing herself up again. But she can't. She is sinking back into the muddy ground. Curling into a ball.

And that's when she feels the rippling across her back. Feathery and light. Along her cheek and neck. Blowing the tangled hair out of her face.

Breath.

Warm against her skin. Soft, like a kiss.

Shiloh does not know how she knows. But she is safe now. Falling into darkness. Safe.

part four:
Flight

BURDEN, KENTUCKY—*The sheriff and his deputies were dispatched to a farm here during the early hours of the morning in response to a call placed to 911.*

Upon arrival at the DiLima stable, owned by Mrs. Jessalynn DiLima, the police discovered the body of a man whom they have identified as Keeler D. Williams of Loyal County. Williams had suffered a severe blow to the head and was pronounced dead at the scene. A young girl, whose name is being withheld because she is a minor, was taken to the nearby hospital with minor injuries. She is being held for observation.

The case is still under investigation at this time, but one anonymous source stated that Williams had allegedly attacked the girl and was then fatally wounded while attempting to steal a racehorse named Dream of Night from the DiLima property.

Police records show that about twenty-five horses, including Dream of Night, had been removed from Williams two months prior due to allegations of abuse and neglect. As is often the case with such removals, most of the horses had been fostered out to surrounding farms for possible adoption. Williams had filed a suit in county court blocking the adoptions and requesting that the horses be returned to him immediately.

While names and addresses of those who foster horses in such disputed cases are not divulged, the anonymous source said that it appeared Williams had discovered the where-abouts of Dream of Night, and had decided to take matters into his own hands.

According to Tom Evers, assistant director of the Loyal County Humane Society, the sheriff had been called out on numerous occasions to escort Williams from the Humane Society's premises due to threats and intimidating behavior.

Neighbors and acquaintances of Williams stated that he had become increasingly irate over the theft, as he saw it, of his property. He was particularly infuriated by the loss of Dream of Night, a horse he considered to be worth a good deal of money.

Dream of Night is a registered Thoroughbred who had a promising racing career early on but who was plagued by injury and later disappeared from the racing circuit. The horse is a ward of the state pending the results of this inves-tigation.

Mrs. Jessalynn DiLima is well known in the Burden and Loyal County community. She retired several years ago from officially training and boarding horses, but has, according to friends, continued to be active in the rescue and rehabilitation *of abused and mistreated horses in the area. DiLima is also registered with the department of social services as a foster care provider. It is believed that the young girl attacked by Williams is a foster child living in DiLima's home.*

"It was never my mom, was it?"

"No."

"I thought ... There was a phone call. ... I thought ..."

The girl's voice trails off. She is staring at the blank white hospital wall. The bruises are blackish blue around her neck, along one cheek.

"It wasn't ... my mom's boyfriend, either."

"No."

The woman waits. She's not sure what the girl knows. How much she understands.

The doctor said she might not remember everything about that night. Because of the concussion. The sheriff said she seemed confused. About who was actually out in the dark. Some story about waiting for her mom to come get her, about her mom's boyfriend.

And then, of course, there's the suitcase, full of clothes and food. The girl was trying to run away. At least that much is clear.

"Who was it, then?"

"Night's owner. He wanted him back. Thought he'd steal him in the middle of the night, I guess, when he thought nobody'd be around."

"The man's dead, isn't he?"

"Yes," the woman says, thinking it's best to be honest. After everything that's happened.

"What about Night?" The girl's eyes shift from the wall, full of panic, fear. "Is he dead?"

Quickly the woman shakes her head.

"Oh, no. No. Night is fine. He got pretty spooked, but he's fine."

The girl looks away again.

"Night protected you."

The woman leans in closer. She wants to make sure the girl understands.

"Night kept you safe."

The girl scowls.

"It's true. When I heard all the ruckus, I ran outside, and I found Night standing over you. In fact, he didn't want to leave your side."

Still scowling, but wanting to believe. The woman can see it. The girl wants to believe.

"He wouldn't let me anywhere near you at first. Not for a while. But finally he understood. I was there to help."

The girl is taking it in, thinking it over.

"He screamed at you, didn't he?"

There is the usual toughness, but something is shifting. A grin, trying to work its way out.

"Yep, he screamed at me, all right."

Grinning back. A little. Not too much, not yet.

The girl settles her head deeper into the big white pillow, closes her eyes. And the woman leans back too, against the tall hospital chair.

"Oh, Shenandoah, I long to see you,

Away, you rolling river."

The girl's eyelids flutter but they don't open all the way. So the woman keeps on singing, softly, to herself.

"Oh, Shenandoah, I long to see you,

Away, we're bound away, 'cross the wide Missoura."

The woman goes through every verse. She assumes the girl has fallen asleep. So she stops singing when the song ends.

"What's that about, anyway?"

The girl sounds annoyed. Her eyes flash up at the woman.

"A river," the woman answers. She stops to think a moment. "The Shenandoah is a river. But I guess the song's more about a longing for something. A place. A home."

The woman waits, sure the girl will make some smart remark about how dumb the song is, how pointless.

"You can sing it again. If you want."

Not a request. More like a challenge. As if the girl is still ready to pick a fight if she has to.

"Sure."

And so the woman begins to sing, and the girl listens. The same song, all over again.

One

SHILOH

Brrrrrr—

The girl picks up the receiver. She's been waiting. A whole year. And now she's ready.

"Mom."

No click. And so she takes a deep breath. She has a lot to say.

"I'm living on a farm now. I've been here awhile. I didn't like it at first. I didn't like Jess. But now I think she's okay. She's kind of old, like a grandma, but she's teaching me to ride horses. There's this one horse. His name is Night. He lets me brush him now. Which is a really big deal because he used to not let anybody even go near him."

She waits, giving her mom a chance.

"Night's all black. He used to be a racehorse. We rescued him. Well, Jess rescued him. And then I helped. He won't let anybody brush him except me. Well, sometimes he'll let Jess. But he used to scream at her all the time. He used to scream at everybody, except me. It sounds like a person screaming. It really does."

Pausing for air.

"Night protected me. This guy tried to hurt me last year, and Night protected me. I know that sounds weird because he's just a horse. But he's smart. He can sense things. Because this man tried to steal him back, and I was there, so the man attacked me because he was drunk and mean. And Night knew, and he stopped the guy."

Another deep breath.

"And we almost lost Night because of that. People thought he was a dangerous horse. Because he hurt the man, kicked him in the head and killed him just like that. But it was an accident, and Jess made them see. She went to the judge and everything. She made them see. Night was only trying to protect me."

Shiloh stops. She thinks she hears something on the other end. Crying. Is it her little sister crying? How old is her sister now? She can't be a baby anymore.

And then Shiloh knows. It's not a child crying.

"I'm okay, Mom," she says, quiet but firm. The way Jess talks to the horses when they're upset. "I'm okay, really. You don't have to worry about me. And you can still call on my birthday. But you can call some other times too. If you want."

Shiloh's throat is getting tight. Hearing her mom cry like that. But she has more to say.

"I don't know how you get the phone numbers. The state lady says you're not supposed to know. Where I am. She says there's no way you could've had all those numbers, the places I lived. Unless somebody's telling you when they're not supposed to. In the state lady's office. But I'm glad. I'm glad you call sometimes."

Shiloh stops now. Her voice is getting too wobbly. She doesn't want her mom to think she's still a baby. A crybaby. Because she's not. She's one tough cookie. Jess has told her so.

"Happy birthday, Shy."

The voice comes out low and gravelly, like Shiloh remembers. Shiloh presses the phone to her ear. She wants more. Because she loves her mom's voice. The very sound. It would be the best birthday present ever. If her mom just kept on talking.

"I guess I didn't tell you before. Your sister's name is Madison. I call her Maddie."

A slow intake of air, on the other end. A cigarette maybe, or her mom just trying to catch her breath.

"Her middle name is Hope."

Shiloh lets it roll around inside her head.

Madison Hope.

Shiloh Grace.

Sisters.

"Maybe Maddie can come see the horses sometime." Shiloh can't stop herself. The words rush out. "Maybe you could bring her, and you all could meet the horses. And Jess."

Silence.

"Not right now," Shiloh jumps in quickly. "But sometime."

Shiloh waits. And waits. She'll wait forever if she has to. But she hopes she doesn't have to.

"Maybe we will, Shy. Sometime."

More silence, and then the *click*. And the voice is gone. Like it was never there at all. But Shiloh knows. It was.

JESSALYNN

Brrrrnnnnnnng!

The woman is tugged out of sleep. A heavy, dreamless sleep.

Brrrrnnnnnnng!

Because the baby is gone, vanished, like the grandchild that never was.

But that's okay. The woman doesn't need the dream anymore. She doesn't need to keep reaching for something she already has.

Brrrrnnnnnnng!

Jess plucks up the receiver, squints at the numbers on the clock.

"Okay, Nita, what've we got?" she asks instead of saying hello.

"Big emergency. Bunch of horses. I don't know how many. Abandoned by the side of the road. Can you believe it? The sheriff's stopping traffic. I'll pick y'all up in thirty."

Click.

Jess allows herself a couple of minutes, and then slowly, carefully, she pushes herself up and out of bed. Stretching, making her way into her clothes.

Bella's eyes follow the motions, but her body shows no hint of doing the same.

"It's okay, girl." The woman cups her hand under the dog's muzzle. "Stay in bed."

Jess heads down the hall and taps at the bedroom door.

"I heard the phone!" the girl's voice calls right away. "I'm up."

"Nita will be here in about thirty minutes."

"I'll be ready."

In the kitchen Jess starts the coffee, drops a couple of slices of bread into the toaster.

"I'm not hungry," Shiloh says, breathless, as soon as she bursts into the room, pulling on her jacket already.

"It's going to be a long day," Jess warns.

"I know!" A click of the tongue. "You don't have to tell me. I've done this before."

"Once," Jess says, under her breath.

The girl rolls her eyes, but she takes the peanut butter toast, gulping it down as fast as she can.

"I'm going out to check on Night before we go."

Shiloh grabs an apple from the bowl on the counter and tucks it into her jacket pocket.

"Better take more than one of those," Jess gently warns. "Can't be showing up in a barn full of horses with just one apple."

Shiloh clicks her tongue again, but her pockets are full by the time she bangs through the kitchen door.

Jess stands at the counter. She eats a piece of toast, pours out a cup of coffee.

Morning fog is still clinging to the ground outside the window. The day is starting out cold and gray. She'll have to keep moving this morning if she doesn't want to be stiff as a board come tomorrow.

At least now she has somebody to help with the chores. The girl doesn't complain about the manure anymore. She doesn't complain about any of the work, especially if it has to do with horses.

Jess pours the rest of the pot into a thermos for later.

She glances up from the counter just in time to see Shiloh disappear into the barn. Because that's where the black horse is. Now that it's turning chilly at night. Inside his own stall. Right where the girl led him.

NIGHT

Brrrrnnnnnnng!

The sound comes, sudden and sharp. Shrill. Like the call of a bird, but not. The sound is not a living sound. It is only a memory. From long ago. He knows that now.

The sound. The fighting. The roaring.

They are all a part of him. But they are not everything. Not even the pain is everything, the anger. Not anymore.

There is the sun and the grass. And fresh hay and clean water. Every single day.

There is the stall, warm and dry. Walls, yes, but not a prison.

There is the woman who already smells like horses.

And there is the girl who is still angry sometimes, still afraid, but who comes to him. Every day. And who is starting to smell like horses too.

Author's Note

I was inspired to write this story after moving back to my home state of Kentucky, and learning that my neighbor rescued ex-racehorses. Why did ex-racehorses need rescuing? I wondered. And that's where this journey began.

There are 35,000 Thoroughbreds registered with the Jockey Club each year. Only one wins the Kentucky Derby.

What happens to the rest?

Hopefully, a horse that simply isn't fast enough to be a winner, or a horse that gets injured, goes on to find a happy ending off the track. A caring owner, a clean stall, enough food to eat.

Too often, though, it doesn't work out that way.

Each year, *thousands* of ex-racehorses end up mistreated, malnourished, abused. *Thousands* of ex-racehorses end up in "kill pens," a last stop on the way to slaughterhouses.

Luckily, there are lots of people out there (like my neighbor) who care, and lots of ways to help. The Thoroughbred Retirement Foundation is a great place to start. Their website (www.trfinc.org) gives information about how to foster, adopt, or sponsor a Thoroughbred. The website also provides links to local organizations all over the country that rescue all kinds of horses, not just Thoroughbreds, and work to give as many of these noble creatures as possible a happy ending.

In researching this book I spoke to many people about horses. I am especially grateful to Susanna Thomas, director of the Maker's Mark Secretariat Center (www.thoroughbredadoption.com), which is the Thoroughbred Retirement Foundation's showcase adoption facility located at the Kentucky Horse Park in Lexington, Kentucky. Susanna is an extraordinary horsewoman, teacher, and guide, and I am deeply indebted to her for sharing with me a tiny fraction of her vast knowledge of the language of Equus.

I would also like to thank Zoé Strecker, longtime friend and always reliable sounding board, for answering silly questions about horses and other things.

Many thanks to the team at Atheneum: Kiley Frank, Alison Velea, Paul Crichton, Molly McLeod, Justin Chanda, Catharine Sotzing, Michelle Fadlalla, Deb Sfetsios, and Michael McCartney.

And last, but not at all least: Thanks, and so much more, goes to my husband, Tim Ungs, and to my family.